HER
DAUGHTER'S
DREAM

HER
DAUGHTER'S
DREAM

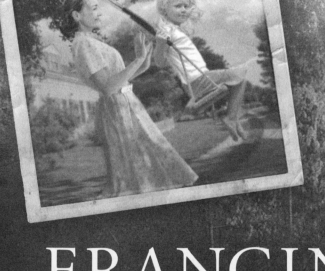

FRANCINE
RIVERS

Tyndale House Publishers, Inc., Carol Stream, Illinois

Visit Tyndale's exciting Web site at www.tyndale.com.

Check out the latest about Francine Rivers at www.francinerivers.com.

TYNDALE and Tyndale's quill logo are registered trademarks of Tyndale House Publishers, Inc.

Her Daughter's Dream

Designed by Beth Sparkman

Edited by Kathryn S. Olson

Published in association with the literacy agency of Browne and Miller Literary Associates, LLC, 410 Michigan Avenue, Suite 460, Chicago, IL 60605.

Unless otherwise indicated, Scripture quotations are taken from the New American Standard Bible,® copyright © 1960, 1962, 1963, 1968, 1971, 1972, 1973, 1975, 1977, 1995 by The Lockman Foundation. Used by permission.

Scripture quotations in chapter 41 are taken from the *Holy Bible*, New Living Translation, copyright © 1996, 2004, 2007 by Tyndale House Foundation. Used by permission of Tyndale House Publishers, Inc., Carol Stream, Illinois 60188. All rights reserved.

Library of Congress Cataloging-in-Publication Data

Rivers, Francine, date.
  Her daughter's dream / Francine Rivers.
    p. cm. — (Marta's legacy ; 2)
  ISBN 978-1-4143-3409-7
  1. Mothers and daughters—Fiction. 2. Self-actualization (Psychology) in women—Fiction.
3. Domestic fiction. I. Title.
  PS3568.I83165H46 2010
  813′.54—dc22   2010020821

ISBN 978-1-4143-3684-8 (International Trade Paper Edition)

Printed in the United States of America

16　15　14　13　12　11　10
7　6　5　4　3　2　1

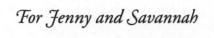

For Jenny and Savannah

Acknowledgments

Most of the novel you are about to read is purely fictional, though there are bits and pieces of personal family history woven throughout. The manuscript has taken various forms over the last two years, and in the end morphed into a saga. Many people have helped me in the process of writing the stories of Marta and Hildemara in the first volume and Carolyn and May Flower Dawn in the second. I want to thank each and every one of them.

First of all my husband, Rick, has ridden the storm through this one, listening to every variation of the stories as the characters took form in my imagination and acting as my first editor.

Every family needs a historian, and my brother, Everett, has played that role to perfection. He sent me hundreds of family pictures that helped flesh out the story. I also received invaluable help from my cousin Maureen Rosiere, who described in detail our grandparents' almond and wine-grape ranch, a pattern I used in this novel. Both my husband and my brother shared their Vietnam experiences with me.

Kitty Briggs, Shannon Coibion (our daughter), and Holly Harder shared their experiences as military wives. Holly has been a constant help to me. I know of no other person on the planet who can find information on the Internet faster! Whenever I ran into a wall, Holly tore it down. Thanks, Holly!

Holly's son, U.S. Army Lieutenant Daniel Harder, gave me information on the engineering and ROTC programs at Cal Poly. He is now on active duty. Our prayers are with him.

Ila Vorderbrueggen, a nurse and personal friend of my mother's, helped me fill in information about long-term patient care in the Arroyo del Valle Sanatorium. I've enjoyed our correspondence.

Kurt Thiel and Robert Schwinn answered questions about Inter-Varsity Christian Fellowship. Keep up the good work, gentlemen!

Globus tour guide Joppy Wissink rerouted a bus so that Rick and I had the opportunity to walk around my grandmother's hometown of Steffisburg, Switzerland.

All along the course of this project, I have had brainstorming partners when I needed them. Colleen Phillips raised questions and encouraged me from the beginning. Robin Lee Hatcher and Sunni Jeffers jumped in with ideas and questions when I didn't know which way to go. My agent, Danielle Egan-Miller, and her associate, Joanna MacKenzie, helped me see how to restructure the novel to show the story I wanted to tell.

I would also like to thank Karen Watson of Tyndale House Publishers for her insights and encouraging support. She helped me see my characters more clearly. And, of course, every writer needs a good editor. I am blessed with one of the best, Kathy Olson. She makes revision work exciting and challenging rather than painful.

Finally, I thank the Lord for my mother and grandmother. Their lives and Mom's journals first inspired the idea of writing about mother-daughter relationships. They were both hardworking women of faith. They both passed on some years ago, but I cling to the promise that they are still very much alive and undoubtedly enjoying one another's company. One day I will see them again.

January 1951

Dear Rosie,

Trip called. Hildemara is back in the hospital. She had been there for nearly two months before they got around to telling me about it. But now they want my help. My sweet Hildemara Rose, the smallest, the weakest, the most dependent of my children. She has struggled from the beginning. And now, somehow, I must find a way to give her the courage for one more struggle.

I didn't always see it, but recently the Lord has reminded me of all the times Hildemara's courage and spunk have served her well. She chose her own path in life and pursued it against all odds (and against my advice, I might add!). She followed that husband of hers from one military base to another, finding apartments in strange cities, making new friends. She crossed the country by herself and came home to help Bernhard and Elizabeth hold on to the Musashis' land, despite threats and fire and bricks through their windows.

And I needn't remind you of her response when faced with the same kind of abuse that our dear Elise succumbed to so many years ago. She was smart enough to run. My daughter has courage!

I have been forced to admit that I have always favored Hildemara a little above the others. (Is any of this news to you, my dear friend? I suspect you know me better than I know myself.) From the moment my first daughter came into the world, she has held a special place in my heart. Niclas always said she looked like me, and I'm afraid it's true. And we both know how little regard my father had for my plain looks. And like Elise, she was frail.

How could a mother's heart fail to respond to such a combination? I did what I felt I had to do. From the start I determined that I would not cripple Hildemara Rose the way Mama crippled Elise. But now I wonder if I did the right thing. Did I push her too hard and, in so doing, push her away? She wouldn't even let her husband call me for help until they both thought she was past the point of no return. I wish now I'd been more like my mother, with her gracious and loving spirit, and less like my father. Yes, that's right. I see clearly that I inherited some of his selfish and cruel ways. Don't try to convince me otherwise, Rosie. We both know it's true.

Now my hope and prayer is that I can bring Hildemara close again. I am praying for more time. I want Hildemara to know how much I love her, how proud I am of her and her accomplishments. I want to mend my relationship with her. I want to learn how to serve my daughter. I, who have rebelled all my life at the very thought of servanthood.

I started thinking about Lady Daisy and our afternoons at Kew and tea in the conservatory. I think it's about time I shared some of these experiences with Hildemara Rose. . . . I will make all the wonderful sweets and savories for Hildemara Rose that I once served to Lady Daisy. I will pour India tea and lace it with cream and conversation.

God willing, I will win back my daughter.

Your loving friend,
Marta

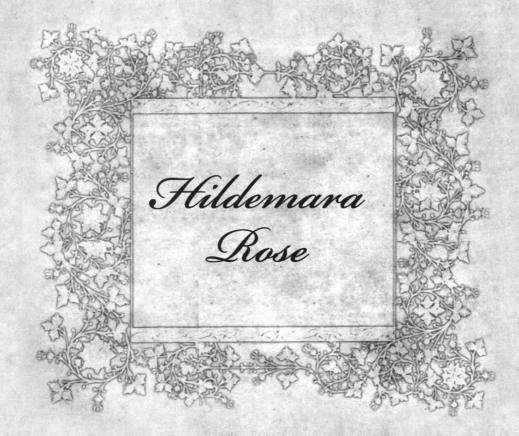

Hildemara Rose

HILDEMARA LAY IN the darkness, her nightgown damp with perspiration. Night sweats again—she should be used to them by now. Her roommate, Lydia, snored softly. Lydia had been steadily improving since she arrived six weeks ago, which only served to depress Hildemara more. Lydia had gained two pounds; Hildie lost the same amount.

Two months and still no improvement, hospital bills mounting daily, crushing Trip's dreams beneath their weight. Her husband came each afternoon. He'd looked so tired yesterday, and no wonder when he had to work full-time and then go home and take care of all her duties: laundry, cooking, seeing to Charlie's and Carolyn's needs. Hildie grieved over her children—Charlie on his own so much of the time, Carolyn being raised by an indifferent babysitter. She hadn't touched or seen her children since Trip brought her to the hospital. She missed them so much, she felt physical pain most of the time. Or was that just the *mycobacterium tuberculosis* consuming her lungs and decimating her body?

Pushing the covers back, Hildie went to the bathroom to rinse

her face with cool water. Who was that gaunt, pale ghost staring
back at her in the mirror? She studied the sharp angles, the pallor,
the shadows beneath her hazel eyes, the lackluster brown color of
the hair around her shoulders.

*I'm dying, Lord, aren't I? I haven't enough strength to fight this
disease. And now I have to face Mama's disappointment in me. She
called me a coward last time. Maybe I am giving up.* She cupped
water in her hands and pressed her face into it. *Oh, God, I love Trip
so much. And Charlie and sweet little Carolyn. But I'm tired, Lord, so
very tired. I'd rather die now, than linger and leave a legacy of debt.*

She'd told Trip as much last week. She only wished she could
die at home, rather than in a sterile hospital room twenty miles
away. His face had twisted in anguish. "Don't say that. You're not
going to die. You have to stop worrying about the bills. If your
mother came, I could bring you home. Maybe then . . ."

She'd argued. Mama wouldn't come. She'd never helped before.
Mama hated the very idea of being a servant. And that's exactly
what she'd be—a full-time maid and washerwoman, babysitter
and cook, without pay. Hildie said she couldn't ask such a thing
of Mama.

Trip called Mama anyway, and then he went down on Saturday
with Charlie and Carolyn so he and Mama could talk things over.
He'd come out this morning. "Your mother said yes. I'm taking
a couple of days off to get things ready for her." He wanted to
repaint Carolyn's room, buy a nice, comfortable bed, a new dresser
and mirror, maybe a rocking chair. "Charlie and Carolyn will have
the small bedroom. You and I'll be together. . . ."

"I can't sleep with you, Trip. I need to be quarantined." She
could barely absorb the news that Mama had agreed to help. "I
can't be near the children." At least, she could hear them; she could
see them. Mama said she'd come. Mama was moving in. Hildie
trembled, taking it all in. She felt a little sick to her stomach. "I'll
need a hospital bed." She gave Trip instructions about her room.
No rug. A window shade rather than curtains. The simpler the
room, the easier to keep sanitized. Trip looked so hopeful, it broke

her heart. He leaned down to kiss her forehead before he left. "You'll be home soon."

Now, she couldn't sleep. Rather than get back into bed, Hildie sat in a chair by the window and looked out at the stars. What was it going to be like, having Mama living under her roof, taking care of her, taking care of her children, taking care of all the chores that needed to be done so Trip didn't have to do everything? Would Mama despise her for not fighting harder? Her eyes burned; her throat ached just thinking about having to lie in bed sick and helpless while Mama took over her family. She wiped tears away. Of course, Mama would do it all better than she ever could. That realization hurt even more. Mama had always managed everything. Even without Papa, the ranch ran like a well-oiled machine. Mama would fix Trip wonderful meals. Mama would be the one to give Charlie wings. Mama would probably have Carolyn reading before she turned four.

I should be grateful. She cares enough to come and help. I didn't think she did.

When the night air had cooled her, Hildie slipped beneath the covers again.

She wanted to be grateful. She would say thank you, even as she had to watch the life she loved slip away from her. She had fought hard to be free of Mama's expectations, to claim her own life and not live out her mother's impossible dreams. Even the one thing at which she'd excelled would be stripped from her before she closed her eyes for the last time.

Mama would be the nurse. Mama would carry the lantern.

Carolyn

2

Carolyn was happy that Daddy let her stay with Oma Marta in Murietta until Oma was ready to move to their house. If she had gone home with him and Charlie, she would have had to go to Mrs. Haversal's across the street every day while Charlie was at school and Daddy went to work. It had been like that for a long time, ever since Mommy went away. But now, Mommy was coming home and Oma was coming to stay. It would be wonderful!

Carolyn played with the rag doll Oma had given her, while Oma packed her suitcase with clothing and a trunk with sheets, crochet-trimmed and embroidered pillowcases, two blankets, and a pink rose tea set with tiny silver spoons. Oma put the suitcase and trunk in the back of her new gray Plymouth, and then she stacked two cushions in the front seat so Carolyn could sit high up and see out the window on the long drive home. Oma even let her roll her window down so she could put her hand out and feel the air.

They pulled into the driveway just when Charlie got off the school bus. "Oma!" He came running. Oma took the front door key out from under the flowerpot on the front porch.

Everything had changed inside the house. Carolyn found her bed and dresser in Charlie's room.

A small table stood between Charlie's bed and hers. She went back to her old room and watched Oma swing her suitcase onto a new, bigger bed. The pink walls were now bright yellow, and new lacy white curtains hung over the windows. There was a big dresser with a mirror on top, a little table and lamp, and a rocking chair with flowered cushions.

"I'm going to be very comfortable here." Oma unpacked her clothes and put them away.

Oma stepped to the window and drew the white lacy curtains aside. "I'm going to have to get used to having neighbors this close." She shook her head and turned away. "I'd better get dinner started. Your daddy will be coming home soon."

"Is Mommy coming home?"

"In another day or two." Oma opened the door into the spare bedroom. "This is where she'll be." Leaving Carolyn in the bedroom doorway, Oma headed for the kitchen. Carolyn didn't like the room. It felt cold and strange without a rug on the floor and no curtains on the window, just a shade pulled down to block out the sunlight.

Carolyn came into the kitchen. "Mommy isn't going to like her room."

"It's exactly the way she wants it. Easy to keep clean."

"Mommy likes plants on the windowsill. She likes flowers in a vase." Mommy always had pictures in frames on her dresser.

"Mommy doesn't like germs." Oma peeled potatoes.

"What are germs?"

Oma chuckled. "You'll have to ask your mother."

Oma had dinner ready before Daddy came home from work. They all sat around the kitchen table. "When do you pick her up?" Oma set a pitcher of milk on the table and sat in Mommy's chair.

"Day after tomorrow."

"Plenty to be thankful for, haven't we?" When Oma stretched out her hands, Charlie took one and Carolyn the other. Daddy took their hands too so they made a circle. He hadn't said grace since Mommy went away. He spoke quietly now, calmly, said *amen* and sighed, a smile tugging at his lips. Oma asked questions about his work, and Daddy talked for a long time. When everyone had finished dinner, Daddy stacked the dishes, but Oma shooed him away. "You and the kids go visit or play or whatever you normally do. I'll take care of cleaning up."

Daddy took Charlie outside to play catch. Carolyn sat on the front steps and watched.

Oma handled the baths that night, Charlie first so he could do his homework. She sat on the closed toilet while Carolyn played in the bubble bath. Oma gave Daddy a book to read to them, with Carolyn on one side and Charlie on the other. When he finished, he kissed them both and sent them to bed. Oma tucked them in with prayers.

In the middle of the night, Carolyn awakened. She'd gotten used to sleeping with Oma. Charlie didn't have monsters in his room, but Carolyn worried about Oma. Crawling out of bed, she crept down the hall to her old bedroom and opened the door. Oma snored so loudly, she'd probably scared all the monsters out of the house with the noise she made. Scampering back to Charlie's room, Carolyn dove into bed. Snuggling down into the covers, she looked at Charlie sleeping on the other side of the room, thought of Mommy coming home, and went to sleep smiling.

❆ ❆ ❆

Daddy left for work right after a breakfast of scrambled eggs, bacon, and fresh-baked biscuits. As soon as Charlie left for school, Oma tipped Carolyn's chin. "Let's go brush your hair and put it in a ponytail. What do you say?" She took Carolyn by the hand and led her into her bedroom. She patted the bed and Carolyn climbed up onto it. While Oma brushed her hair, Carolyn watched her grandmother in the mirror. She liked her white hair and tanned, wrinkled cheeks. She had warm green-brown eyes like Mommy's.

Oma smiled back at her. She brushed Carolyn's long, curly blonde hair into her hand. "You look like Elise. She was my little sister, and she was very, very pretty, just like you." When all the tangles had been worked out, Oma wound a rubber band around Carolyn's hair. "There. That looks better. Don't you think?"

Carolyn looked up. "Is Mommy dying?"

Oma smiled at Carolyn. "No. Your mother is *not* dying." She ran her hand over Carolyn's hair. "She needs rest. That's all. Now that I'm here, she can come home and rest. You'll see your mother every day."

Carolyn didn't see the mixture of emotions in Oma's face that she had seen in Daddy's. Oma didn't look uncertain or sad. She didn't look afraid. Oma wore glasses, but behind them Carolyn saw clear, warm eyes filled with confidence.

Oma told Carolyn they were going for a ride. "I need to get to know the area, find out where things are."

"What things?"

"Grocery store, for one. You and I are going to explore!" She made it sound like a great adventure. "We're going to find a library, where we can check out enough books to last a week. And I want to stop by the church, meet the pastor. Your daddy said you haven't gone for a while, but that's going to change."

"Will Mommy go, too?"

"No. Not for a while."

Oma drove fast, pointing this way and that, while Carolyn perched on pillows, taking in the sights. "Look over there. What do you know! A cheese factory! We'll pick up some good Swiss or Gouda cheese while we're in town. And there's a bank."

Oma took her to lunch at a small café on Main Street. Carolyn ate a hot dog and drank Coke. Before heading home, Oma wanted to wander through a department store. She looked through all the kitchen gadgets and bought a few. Then they went to the grocery store, and Oma filled the big basket. "Time to head home. We want to be there when Charlie gets off the bus."

Oma pulled into the driveway just as the school bus disgorged boys and girls. "Perfect timing!" Charlie ran up the street, whooping. Oma laughed and told him he sounded like a wild Indian. She handed him a bag of groceries. "You can help unload." She gave a smaller bag to Carolyn and carried in another bag and the package from the department store.

Charlie sniffed out the package of Fig Newtons like a bloodhound, opened it, grabbed a handful, and headed out the door to find his friends. Amused, Oma shook her head. "He's like one of my Summer Bedlam boys." Oma tore brown paper from the package and opened a big white box. "Look what I found when we were out shopping." She laid out a small embroidered tablecloth and matching napkins. "You and I and Mommy are going to make high tea every afternoon. It's been years since I've done it, but I have all the recipes right here." She took a worn leather book from her purse and set it on the table. She got a dreamy look on her face. "We're going to make this a special homecoming." She glanced at her watch and suggested they sit on the porch and enjoy the sunshine.

❄ ❄ ❄

When Daddy brought Mommy home, Oma stood, holding Carolyn's hand. Mommy climbed out of the car, waved hello, and went straight into the house. Carolyn called out to her and followed them inside, but her father blocked her. "Leave your mother alone. She's going to bed." Mommy went down the hall into the cold room with the strange bed and closed the door. When Carolyn tried to go around Daddy, he caught hold of her and turned Carolyn around. "Go play outside for a while so Oma and I can talk. Go on now." He gave her a push.

Confused, Carolyn sat on the front steps until Daddy came out. He went right past her, got back into his car, and drove away.

Oma came out onto the front porch. "Your daddy had to go back to work. You'll see him this afternoon."

"Can I see Mommy?"

"No, *Liebling*." She shook her head and ran her hand over

Carolyn's head. "Do you want to stay out here or come inside and help me make lunch?" Carolyn followed Oma back inside.

Her mother didn't come out of her room at all that day, except to use the bathroom. And every day after that was the same way. If she saw Carolyn in the hallway, she waved her away. Mommy didn't sit at the kitchen table for dinner or with the family in the living room when they listened to *Lux Radio Theater*. No one except Daddy and Oma could go into Mommy's room. Daddy often spent all evening behind the closed door while Oma took a book from the pile she'd checked out of the library and read stories to Carolyn and Charlie.

Carolyn often went outside after Charlie went to school. One day she picked daffodils that had sprouted up from bulbs Mommy had planted a long time ago. Mommy loved flowers. They made her happy. When Carolyn had a fistful, she went inside, crept along the corridor to Mommy's room, and opened the door. Mommy lay on her side, sleeping. Carolyn tiptoed to the bed. She stood chin level with the top of the mattress.

"Mommy?" Reaching up, Carolyn touched her mother's hand. Her mother's eyes flickered open. A smile curved her mouth. Carolyn held up the daffodils. "I brought you flowers, Mommy, to make you feel better."

Mommy's expression changed. Pulling up the sheet, she covered her mouth. "You're not supposed to come in here, Carolyn. Go! Now!"

Her lip trembled. "I want to be with you."

"You can't be with me." Her mother's eyes filled with tears. "Get out of here, Carolyn. Do what you're told."

"Mommy . . ." Carolyn reached out to give her the flowers.

Her mother reared back. "Mama!" Mommy started to cough. "Get away from me!" she choked out between coughs. When Oma appeared in the doorway, Mommy waved frantically. "Mama! Get her out of here! Get her away from me!" Sobbing now, still coughing, Mommy bunched the sheet over her mouth and hunched over. "Keep her out!"

Oma hustled Carolyn out of the room and closed the door
firmly. Frightened, confused, Carolyn wailed. Oma picked her up
and carried her into the living room. "Hush now! You didn't do
anything wrong. Listen to me." She sat in the rocker. "Mommy's
sick. You can't go in that room. If you do, she'll go away again. You
don't want that, do you?"

"No." Why couldn't she go in? Oma did. Daddy did. Charlie
stood in the doorway and talked to Mommy. Why did she have to
stay away?

"Shhhh . . ." Oma lifted Carolyn into her lap and rocked her.
Carolyn stuck her thumb in her mouth and leaned against her
grandmother. "Everything is going to be fine, *Liebling*. Your mother
is going to get better. You'll have plenty of time with her then."

Carolyn never went into Mommy's room after that. The closest
she came was standing against the wall outside the door when Oma
took in a tray of food. She could catch a glimpse of Mommy then.
When the weather warmed, her mother came out of her room
wearing a pair of slacks and a sweater. She sat on the front porch,
where Oma served tea, egg salad and dill sandwiches, and pecan
cookies. Carolyn waited inside until Oma told her she could come
out, too. She sat in the chair on the farthest end of the porch as far
away from her mother as she could get. Her mother drew the blue
sweater more tightly around her thin body. "It's cold."

Oma poured tea. "It's seventy-three degrees, Hildemara Rose.
You need fresh air."

"It's hard to keep warm even with the sun shining, Mama."

"I'll get you a blanket." Oma put another sandwich on
Mommy's plate.

"No blanket, Mama. It's better if we try to look as normal as
possible."

"Normal? The neighborhood already knows, Hildemara Rose.
Why do you think they all stay away?" Oma gave a tight laugh.
"Cowards! The lot of them."

Mommy nibbled at the small sandwich. "You're a wonderful
cook, Mama."

"I learned from the best." Oma set her teacup in its saucer. "I learned from Rosie's mother. They had a hotel. I've told you that, haven't I? Chef Brennholtz tutored me at the *Hotel Germania*. He returned to Germany and got caught up in the war. Last I heard, he was chef to one of the ranking Nazis. After Warner Brennholtz, I worked for the Fourniers in Montreaux. Solange shared her French recipes. Lady Daisy's cook, Enid, taught me how to make these tea cakes." Oma talked about Lady Daisy's love of Kew Gardens. Oma pushed her in a wheelchair, and they visited the park every day. "It was hard work, but I never minded. I love English gardens. Of course, it's too hot in Murietta. . . ."

Oma and Mommy talked about Carolyn, too. "She needs a playmate."

"Well, the mothers won't want their children having anything to do with her."

"I've been thinking. It might be good to get a puppy."

"A puppy?"

"For Carolyn."

"I don't know, Mama. A dog is a big responsibility."

"It wouldn't hurt her to learn a little. It might make her less dependent." Oma smiled at Carolyn. "She's become my little shadow."

Mommy leaned her head back and closed her eyes. "I'll talk to Trip." She sounded so tired.

That night at the dinner table, Daddy, Oma, and Charlie talked about getting a puppy. Daddy suggested buying a cocker spaniel. "Small enough to live inside the house and big enough that it couldn't squeeze through the fence."

"You don't have to *buy* a dog." Oma gave a short laugh. "People are always trying to give pups away. Any mutt will do."

Charlie groaned loudly. "Not a mutt. Can't we get a German shepherd, Dad?" He'd stayed overnight with a friend whose family had a new television set. "Roy Rogers has a German shepherd. Bullet runs so fast, he's like a streak of lightning."

Oma looked unconvinced. "And where's he going to run? A big dog like that needs space."

Charlie wasn't about to give up. "We've got a yard in front and a yard in back."

Dad kept eating. "I wouldn't have to worry as much with a police dog around. He'd have to be trained, though. I know someone who can give me pointers."

A few days later, Dad lifted a ball of fur with drooping ears and bright brown eyes out of his car. He handed the pup to Carolyn, who snuggled it against her chest. "Hang on. He wiggles a lot. Don't drop him." He laughed as the pup licked Carolyn's face. "I think he likes you."

After that, Carolyn spent most of the day outside with the puppy, which they named Bullet. When she went inside, he sat by the front door and whined until she came back out. Mommy would come out and sit on the porch while Oma worked in the kitchen, and Carolyn ran around the yard, Bullet on her heels, leaping, yipping.

❇ ❇ ❇

Whenever Oma went anywhere, Carolyn went with her. Sometimes they drove as far as the strawberry fields in Niles, where Oma talked with the Japanese farmers and bought flats of fruit to make jam. Other times they went to the cheese factory by the bridge over the creek that ran through Paxtown. Oma would take her into the storage room with the old Greek gentleman, who bored samples from big wheels of cheese while he and Oma talked of their old countries. Oma ran all the errands for the family: she shopped at Hagstrom's grocery store, picked up supplies for repairs at Kohln's Hardware, and bought clothes for Charlie and Carolyn from Doughtery's department store. Sometimes Mommy argued with her about that.

Every Sunday, Oma took Carolyn to the Presbyterian church while Daddy and Mommy and Charlie stayed home. Daddy always said he had work to do, and Charlie stayed home because Daddy did. Once a month, Oma took Carolyn with her to the farm in

Murietta. While Oma talked with the Martins, Carolyn climbed into the tree house or fed carrots to the white rabbit or watched the chickens. Carolyn slept with Oma when they visited the farm.

Carolyn didn't suck her thumb when she slept in Oma's big bed. She curled up against Oma and felt warm and secure. She dreamed about tea parties with the white rabbit that ate carrots from her hand. He stood on his back legs, tapped his foot, and told her he wanted ice cream tomorrow. She giggled in her sleep.

Everything felt good and safe and comfortable.

3

1952

It took almost a year, but Mommy got better, just like Oma said she would. She spent more time out of her room than in it. She sat at the kitchen table with the family, and she spent time in the living room, though she didn't encourage Carolyn to sit beside her or get too close. "Just play on the rug where I can watch you." Charlie built forts with Lincoln Logs; Carolyn colored in her coloring books or sat plastered to Oma's side, listening to another story.

Often at night, Carolyn would hear Mommy and Oma talking. Sometimes they raised their voices.

"I can do the dishes, Hildemara."

"I'm not an invalid anymore."

"Calm down—"

"I don't want to be calm. I don't want to sit by and see you do everything for Trip and my children. I'm strong enough now to do some of the work around here."

"I'm trying to help!"

"You've helped enough, Mama. Sometimes I think you help too much."

Once Carolyn overheard Daddy. "That's between you and your mother. Stop complaining! She saved us, Hildie. We'd be further in debt than we are now if she hadn't come and helped us out."

"That doesn't mean it can go on like this forever, Trip. This is *my* family. Mine!"

"You're being ridiculous."

"You don't see what I see. I'm losing—"

"It isn't a contest."

"You don't understand!"

Carolyn became frightened when her parents fought. She stuck closer to Oma, hoping she'd never leave.

Mommy moved back into Daddy's big bedroom. A truck came and took away the hospital bed and rolling tray table. Mommy scrubbed the floors and walls and painted the room pink. Daddy moved Carolyn's furniture in. Oma found a round braided rug and trunk for her toys, and she bought fabric with flowers all over it and made curtains.

Bullet jumped the fence and chased the mailman. The poor dog had to be on a chain after that. Daddy built a house big enough for him and Carolyn to sit inside.

Oma said having a room all your own was a luxury, but Carolyn didn't like being in a room by herself. She was afraid the monsters would move in under her bed again.

When Oma packed her suitcase, Carolyn watched, confused. "Where are you going?"

"Murietta."

Carolyn went back to her room and packed her little suitcase, too, just like she always did when Oma took her down to Murietta for a weekend at the farm.

"You're not going with me, Carolyn." Oma sat on her bed and lifted Carolyn to her knee. "You're going to stay here with your mommy."

"I want to go with you."

"You belong here."

"No, I don't."

Oma hugged her and kissed the top of her head. "I hope I haven't stayed too long." She set Carolyn on her feet. "You be a good girl for your mother."

"I love *you*."

Oma cupped her face and kissed each of her cheeks. "I love you, too, *Liebling*. Don't you ever forget that." She stood and took Carolyn's hand. "Come on, now."

Everyone stood outside on the porch. Oma said good-bye, giving each of them a hug and kisses on both cheeks, all except Mommy, who wouldn't let her. "Have it your way, Hildemara Rose." Oma shook her head as she went down the front steps. Carolyn tried to follow. Mommy clamped hold of her shoulders and pulled her back.

"No!" Carolyn struggled, but Mommy's hands tightened, her fingers digging in painfully. Carolyn screamed. "Oma! *Oma!*"

Oma turned her head away, backed out of the driveway, and started down the street. Thrashing, sobbing, Carolyn tried to break free. "Stop it," Mommy said in a broken voice.

Daddy caught Carolyn by the arm and slung her around. He shoved her inside the front door. When she tried to run out, he lifted her under his arm and carried her kicking and screaming down the hall. "*Stop it!* You upset your mother!" Cursing, he flipped Carolyn over his knees and whacked her twice, hard. The pain shocked and frightened her into silence. Daddy flung her onto the bed. Face red, eyes black, he bent over her, a finger pointing at the middle of her face. "You move and I'll give you the spanking of your life!"

Daddy's hand trembled. "I don't want to hear you cry again. Do you understand me? No more tears! You think you have it tough? I saw kids half your age in bombed-out buildings, scrambling for something to eat. They didn't have mothers who loved them or took care of them. Their mothers had been blown to bits! Oma's gone home. Life goes on. You make your mother cry and I swear I'll . . ." He made a fist.

Daddy's face changed. He ran a hand over his face and left the room.

❄ ❄ ❄

The door opened, awakening Carolyn. She stuck her thumb in her mouth, her heart beating wildly. She hadn't budged from where Daddy had put her. Not even when she needed to go to the bathroom.

Mommy stood in the doorway. She grimaced. "You had an accident, didn't you?"

Carolyn scooted back on the fouled bed, shaking violently.

"It's all right." Mommy pushed the door wider. "Everything's going to be all right." Her mother didn't come into the room. "No one's mad at you." She spoke at a distance. "Trip!" Her mother's voice broke.

When she heard her father's footsteps, Carolyn scrambled back farther, all the way to the wall. Tears ran down her cheeks. Mommy was upset again, and Daddy would be mad. Carolyn remembered Daddy's face, his fist, and his promise. When Daddy appeared in the doorway, she took little gulping breaths.

"She needs a bath." Mommy wiped tears from her cheeks. "A warm bath, Trip, and talk quietly. She looks like she's in shock." Mommy spoke in a choked voice. "I'll strip the bed and wash everything."

Carolyn didn't remember how she got from the bed to the bath. Daddy showered her first and then put a capful of bubble bath in the tub and filled it with warm water. He talked in a happy voice, but he didn't look happy. His hands shook as he washed her. Despite the warm water, Carolyn shivered all over. When he lifted her out, she stood still while he toweled her dry and dressed her in pajamas.

"You're going to use a sleeping bag tonight. Won't that be fun? You'll be snug as a bug in a rug."

She wanted Oma, but she didn't dare say so. She wanted Bullet, but she didn't think Daddy would let her sleep in the dog's cozy little house. She wanted Charlie.

The radio played in the living room. Daddy tried to untangle her hair. "Mommy is making a nice dinner for us. You tell her how good it is. You say thank you." He gave up on her hair and tossed the brush into the sink. The sound made Carolyn jump. Turning her, he lifted her to his knee and pressed her head against his shoulder. "I know you're going to miss Oma, Carolyn, but you're our little girl." She sat limp, hands like dead spiders in her lap. If she moved, would Daddy hit her again? He set her on her feet. "Go on in the living room." He spoke gruffly. She went quickly. Before going through the doorway, she looked back.

Daddy sat on the closed toilet lid, his head in his hands.

❄ ❄ ❄

Carolyn did everything Mommy and Daddy told her. She didn't question; she didn't argue. Sometimes, after everyone had gone to bed, she would open her bedroom door and creep down the hallway to Charlie's room and sleep curled up in a blanket by his bed. On cold nights, he let her snuggle with him. Sometimes she awakened early enough to go back to her own bed so Mommy wouldn't know she slept in Charlie's room.

The family went to church every Sunday. Carolyn liked Sunday school. The nice teachers read the same stories Oma had. She liked to hear the singing coming through the wall from the sanctuary and wished she could sit in there with its long red carpet and high ceiling and steps leading up to the cross with gold candlesticks and white candles flickering on the table.

One day after church, Daddy turned the car in the opposite direction from home. "I think I've found the place." Daddy smiled at Mommy. Charlie sat tall, peering out the window. Carolyn couldn't see anything.

Daddy turned off the road. The car bounced and jostled. "This is it."

"Look at that tree!" Charlie rolled his window down. "Can I climb it?"

Daddy stopped the car. "Go ahead."

Mommy protested. "It's too tall."

"He'll be fine, Hildie."

"Be careful!" Mommy called after Charlie.

Daddy laughed. "Relax. He's a monkey."

Mommy looked back as Daddy drove on. "An English walnut tree. We could probably get enough nuts off that one tree to pay part of the property taxes."

Daddy grinned. "Just like you to be so practical." He stopped and got out of the car. "Come on. Let's walk the property. See what you think of it."

Carolyn got out after they walked away. She looked for a big tree and spotted her brother high among the branches. Walking back, she stood near the trunk and looked up. Charlie straddled a high branch. She wandered back and heard Mommy and Daddy talking.

"Can we do this, Trip? I mean, neither of us knows anything about building a house."

"We can learn. I've already ordered books from the library. The bank will loan us enough to buy the property. We haven't the money to hire an architect or contractor. We'll have to do it ourselves, Hildie."

"You really want this, don't you, Trip?"

"Don't you? You're the one who says she misses having space around. You talk about the farm all the time."

"Do I?"

Daddy took her hand and kissed it. Drawing it through his arm, they walked together. Carolyn followed far enough behind not to be noticed, close enough to hear. "Just think about it, Hildie. We could stake out the house wherever we want it, hire someone to dig a well. We'd build a shed first to hold whatever tools I'd need to get started. Having a shed would save time in hauling everything back and forth. We could come out a couple times a week after I get off work, get started on the foundations, work weekends. Nothing fancy, just a simple house; one big room to start, add the kitchen next and a bathroom. As soon as we move in, we can add on two more bedrooms."

"You're talking about an awful lot of work, Trip."

"I know, but we'd be building something for ourselves. How else are we going to have our dream home in the country unless we do it?"

"It's a long way from town and schools."

"Only two miles, and there's a school bus. I already checked about that. All Charlie has to do is walk to the end of the driveway. He'll be picked up and dropped off every day."

Mommy looked around again, frowning this time. "I don't know, Trip."

Daddy turned her to face him. "Breathe the air, Hildemara." He slid his hands up and down her arms. "Aren't you tired of living in a house closed in on all sides by other houses? and gossiping neighbors who avoid you like the plague? Wouldn't you like our children to grow up the way you did? in the country with space around them? They'd be safe and free to roam out here. No more living in the shadow of a federal prison."

Stepping away, Mommy bent down and picked up a handful of soil. She smelled it and crumbled the dirt in her hand, letting it sift through her fingers. "Smells good." She brushed off her hands. "We could build a tent-house to start, use a Coleman stove, keep supplies in the trunk of the car, dig a hole, and build an outhouse."

Daddy grinned. "Now you're talking!"

"We could put an orchard of walnut trees up front, plant fruit trees, a few grapevines, and a vegetable garden over there. We could have chickens . . ."

Daddy pulled her into his arms and kissed her. When he drew back, Mommy's face looked pink. Daddy smiled and took her hand. "Let's figure out where to put the house."

Carolyn watched them walk away. She wandered back to the walnut tree and watched her brother climb from one branch to another.

Mommy and Daddy called out. "Charlie! Carolyn! Come on, you two. Time to go home and have lunch." Carolyn climbed into the backseat. Charlie sounded winded from his fast climb down and run to the car. Daddy started the car. "We're going to build a house here, kids. What do you think about that?"

"We're going to live out here?" Charlie sounded worried.

"Yes."

"But what about my friends? If we move, I'll never see them."

"You'd see them in school." Daddy turned onto the road. "And Happy Valley Road has plenty of kids. I saw one riding a bicycle and another one riding a horse."

"A horse?" Charlie's eyes brightened. "Can we get a horse?"

Daddy laughed and glanced at Mommy. "Maybe. But not right away."

No one asked Carolyn what she thought about moving away from the only house she had ever known. Carolyn had no friends or playmates. Only one thing worried her. "Will Oma know how to find me?"

Mommy and Daddy exchanged a look. "Of course." Daddy nodded. Mommy stared out the window.

❄ ❄ ❄

Every Friday after work, Carolyn's father drove the family out to "the property." They went through Paxtown with its Old West buildings, through meadows, and over a hill with a cemetery. Happy Valley Road was the first left on the other side of the hill. Dad had set up a tent-house. Charlie would take off to climb the big walnut tree; Mom laid out sleeping bags on the platforms, set up the Coleman stove, and started dinner. Dad's first project was to dig a deep hole and build an outhouse. Next, he built a shed for his tools and put a heavy padlock on the door.

Left on her own, Carolyn wandered with Bullet. When he scared a man's sheep, Dad drove a steel stake deep into the ground and attached a chain to it. After that, Bullet could only walk in circles. He'd run until he wound himself tight, and Carolyn would walk him in circles the other way until he had more freedom.

Charlie knew everyone on the road within a few weeks. He took Carolyn over to meet their next-door neighbor. Lee Dockery had beehives behind his house. "Call me Dock." He leaned down, smiling at her. "'Hickory, dickory, dock, the mouse ran up the clock.'" His fingers walked from her stomach up her chest and tickled her under the chin. She giggled. He said she could come over anytime and gave them each a honeycomb dripping with sweetness.

Her father told her to stay out of the way. Her mother told her to try not to get so dirty. With Charlie gone most of the time, Carolyn had no one. She often went over to the barbed-wire fence and watched Dock work among his hives. Bees swarmed around him when he lifted wooden frames filled with honeycombs. "Don't they sting you?" she called.

"Bees are my friends. I never take more than they're willing to share."

Dock invited her inside his house and let her spin honey from the combs. He let her dip her finger into the thick, rich, sweet-smelling mass dripping down a tube into glass jars. He called her "honeybee" and petted her head the same way she petted Bullet. Often, he lifted her onto his lap and talked about his wife who had died and how much they had wanted to have children and couldn't. "You look sleepy." He let her rest her head against his chest. He smelled of tobacco and sweat. He stroked her legs under her dress. "Your mother is calling for you." Dock lifted her and set her on her feet. "You have to go home now, honeybee." He kissed her on the mouth and looked so sad. "Come back real soon, and we'll play some games together."

Carolyn ducked under barbed wire stretched between fence posts and ran through the mustard flowers.

"Why didn't you answer me?" Her mother shook her. "Where were you?"

"At Dock's."

"Dock?"

"Mr. Dockery, Mom." Charlie answered for her. "The bee man. He gives us honeycombs." He sat at the makeshift table where the family ate their meals. "He's really nice."

Frowning, her mother let go of her and straightened, looking toward the house next door. "Well, you leave Mr. Dockery alone. I'm sure he has work to do and doesn't need you underfoot."

Carolyn didn't tell her that Dock liked her more than Daddy or Mommy. He said he wanted her to come back and play real soon.

ALL THAT SUMMER, the family still lived in the rental house near the penitentiary during the week and spent weekends on their new property. Neither Daddy nor Mommy read stories or played games anymore. Her father read big books that came in the mail. He made notes and drawings on yellow legal pads. He rolled out white paper and used a ruler to make bigger drawings with numbers all over. Her mother had housework and laundry and the garden. Charlie had friends. Carolyn played alone. She always had the first bath while Charlie listened to a radio program. She was always first in bed, first with the lights out.

Curling on her side, the rag doll tucked tight against her, Carolyn remembered riding around with Oma in the gray Plymouth. She missed opening a package of Wonder bread and eating fresh slices on the way home from the grocery store. She missed having stories read to her and working puzzles on a board Oma kept under her bed. She missed helping in the kitchen and having tea parties in the afternoon. Most of all, she missed Oma's hugs and kisses. Her mother didn't hug or kiss anyone except Daddy.

Charlie went off with his friends every morning, and Mommy did chores inside the house. "Go on outside and play, Carolyn." Carolyn made mud cookies alongside the house, baked them on a board, and pretended to feed her rag doll while Bullet sat beside her, head high, ears perked, panting. Anytime anyone came near the gate, he growled and barked. Sometimes he licked Carolyn's face, but Mommy didn't like him to kiss her. When he did, she always made Carolyn come in and wash with soap that got in her eyes and burned like fire.

She looked forward to Friday night, when Daddy drove them all to the property. Saturday, while her parents poured and smoothed concrete foundations and framed walls, Carolyn went over to Dock's house. When she got sticky, he gave her a bath. He didn't just throw a washcloth to her and tell her to wash herself. He used his hands.

He said he loved her. He said he'd never hurt her.

And she believed him.

❄ ❄ ❄

At the end of the summer, her father finished the big room and the family moved to the property. While Mommy plastered the walls and painted, Daddy started work on the kitchen and bathroom and two bedrooms. Carolyn was glad she would get to share a room with Charlie again. She didn't like sleeping in a room all by herself.

Dock waved Carolyn over when Mommy wasn't looking and invited Carolyn to play when her mother went to work in her garden. He had Chinese checkers and pick-up sticks. He gave her honey and crackers and milk. "Don't tell your mother or father. They'll think you're bothering me and tell you never to visit me again. You want to come back, don't you? You like spending time with old Dock, don't you?"

Wrapping her arms around his neck, Carolyn said she loved him. And she meant it. He always made her go back when

Mommy called. And she knew better than to talk about Dock to anyone.

As soon as Daddy got home, he went to work on the house. The power saw screamed, filling the air with the scent of sawdust, until Mom said dinner was ready.

"You'll be starting school in September, Carolyn," her mother told her. "We're going to orientation day. You'll meet your teacher, Miss Talbot, and learn where to go to catch the school bus home."

Carolyn told Dock she was afraid to go to school. What if nobody liked her? What if the bus left without her? What if . . . ? He lifted her onto his lap and told her everything would be fine. He said he wished she were his little girl. He'd take her away, and she'd never have to go to school. They'd go to Knott's Berry Farm or the San Diego Zoo. He'd take her to the beach and let her play in the sand as long as she wanted. "Would you like to live with me, honeybee?"

"I'd miss Charlie and Oma."

"Charlie has his own friends, and your *oma* hardly ever comes and sees you."

Dock got tired of playing board games. He showed her other games—secret games, he called them, because she was very special. He tied a red silk ribbon around her neck and made a big bow. The first few times, she felt uncomfortable in the pit of her stomach, but he was so nice to her. Gradually, she got over those feelings and did whatever he told her. She didn't want him to stop liking her. Who would be her friend then?

Then one day while they played their secret games, he hurt her. She cried out and Dock clamped his strong, rough hand over her mouth. She tasted blood. Frightened, she struggled, but he held her more firmly. He told her to calm down, to be quiet; everything would be all right; hush now, *hush*!

Then Dock started to cry. "I'm sorry, honeybee. I'm so sorry!" He cried so hard, Carolyn was scared. "I'm sorry. I'm sorry." He washed the blood off her bare legs and put her underwear back on.

He held her between his knees, his face wet and scared. "I can't be your friend anymore, honeybee. And you can't say anything about coming over here. Not to anyone. Not ever. Your mother told you not to come. She'd spank you for disobeying. Your father would shoot me or take me to jail. You don't want that to happen, do you? It'd be your fault." His eyes darted around. "Promise you won't say anything! We'll both get into a lot of trouble if you tell anyone we're friends."

She lay in bed that night, curling on her side, sucking her thumb, still hurting deep inside. Charlie slept like a rock in the other bed. Dock came to her window and tapped softly. Heart pounding, she pretended to be asleep.

The next day, when Dock waved at her, she ducked her head and pretended she didn't see.

He came back again that night and talked softly through the window while Charlie slept. She didn't want to go to Knott's Berry Farm or the San Diego Zoo. She didn't want to go to Mexico. "I'll come back, honeybee. I love you, baby." Shivering, she kept her eyes shut until he went away. She didn't want to play games with him anymore. When all was quiet, she pulled her blanket off the bed, grabbed her pillow, and hid in the closet.

When Charlie slid the door open in the morning, she screamed. He jumped back and screamed, too. Her mother came running in. "What's the matter with you two?"

"Carolyn's in the closet!"

"What are you doing in the closet?"

"I was scared."

"Scared of what?"

She shook her head. She didn't dare tell.

She had nightmares every night. Mommy and Daddy started talking about her in low voices.

"Something's happened to her, Trip. I don't know what, but something's wrong. I feel it. Miss Talbot called this afternoon. She said Carolyn has been falling asleep in the playhouse. Apparently she's sucking her thumb again."

"She hasn't done that in two years."

"Some of the children tease her about it. Miss Talbot tried to talk to her, but she said Carolyn is like a little clam. She hardly talks at all."

Her parents kept looking at her all through dinner. Her father asked if someone was bullying her at school. Her mother said she didn't have to be afraid to tell them anything, but Dock had told her what would happen to her if she did. When she didn't say anything, they asked Charlie. "Have you seen anything going on at school?"

"We're not in the same playground as the little kids."

"What about the school bus?" Dad wanted to know. "Anyone bothering her?"

"I don't know, Dad."

"Well, make it your business to find out." Dad raised his voice. "She's your sister! Watch out for her!"

Tucked in bed for the night and bedroom door closed, Charlie talked to her in the dark. "Tell me who's picking on you, Carolyn. I'll beat 'em up. I'll make them leave you alone." Carolyn thought about how big Dock was, how easily he could hurt her brother. She pulled the blanket over her head and hid under the covers.

When she went to school, Miss Talbot talked with her. "Your mommy says you're having nightmares. Can you tell me about your dreams, sweetheart?" Carolyn shrugged her shoulders and pretended not to remember. Everyone would be mad at her if she said anything about Dock—Mommy, Daddy, Charlie. She had made Dock cry, hadn't she? She had done something terribly wrong.

When Mommy and Daddy started talking about their next-door neighbor, Mr. Dockery, Carolyn felt the terror rise up inside her, catching her by the throat. Her stomach clenched as though Dock were touching her again. She remembered the pain. She remembered the blood. She remembered every word he said. Little yellow and black bees swarmed around her face. She felt cold sensations like insects landing on her and walking around on her skin with little prickly feet.

"I went over this morning, and there are newspapers all over his driveway. He hasn't picked them up in days."

Daddy said something must be wrong, and he'd go over and check on him. Carolyn broke out in a cold sweat while he was gone. He came back and said the mail had piled up by his door, too. He couldn't see anything through the windows. The drapes had been pulled. He made a phone call. Mommy told her to go outside and play when the police came.

Carolyn wanted to run away, but didn't know where to go. She climbed the walnut tree and watched when her father and the other police officer opened the front door of Lee Dockery's house. They came out without him.

Mommy and Daddy talked about Lee Dockery in the living room that evening, after Charlie and Carolyn had been sent to bed. Carolyn got up and sat by the open door, listening.

"We talked with neighbors. No one's seen him in weeks. His truck's gone. So are the beehives. It's like he packed up and took off in a hurry. No one has any idea where he'd go or if he's coming back. They all said he's a strange old bird."

"No one would just walk away from a house and property. Maybe he went to visit relatives."

"No relatives that anyone knows about. I never saw anyone visit. Did you?"

"Charlie and Carolyn went over a few times, but I told them to stay away from him."

"Why?"

"Something about him. I don't know. He gave me the creeps. Trip, you don't suppose . . ." Mommy sounded worried.

"What?"

"Oh, I'm probably overreacting. I just wondered if Carolyn's behavior could have anything to do with him. I did tell her to stay away from him, but what if she didn't?"

Carolyn held her breath. Had they figured out her secret? Would Daddy go after Dock and shoot him, like Dock had said he would?

"Carolyn?" Daddy laughed. "She's much too timid to go visit a strange neighbor without one of us dragging her over there."

Mommy was quiet for a minute. Then she said, "I guess you're right. I just wish I knew what was wrong with her. Trip, she hardly says two words to me. I just don't know what to do anymore."

Then Mommy was crying. Carolyn crept back to bed before she could get into any more trouble than she was already in.

1953

Carolyn's nightmares continued through the winter months but began to lessen as daylight lasted longer. She didn't see as many shadows at night, didn't hear footsteps outside the bedroom window, and didn't have to hide in the closet anymore. She could slip into Charlie's bed. He slept so deeply, he didn't notice until morning.

Dad took time off from building the house to put up a swing. "Might give her something to do. . . ." Carolyn spent hours sitting in the tire seat, turning the ropes until they grew taut, and then lifting her feet off the ground so she'd spin until she felt light-headed and dizzy. Her mother pushed her sometimes. Once, she even sat on the swing herself and showed Carolyn how to pump her legs so she could go higher.

Every few months, Carolyn and Charlie had to go to a hospital for "skin tests." Mom checked their arms every day for a week before taking them back for the doctor to see. When the doctor said, "Negative," Mom smiled and relaxed.

Carolyn made a friend in first grade. New to Paxtown and new to school, Suzie clung to her mother like a limpet and had to be pried off by their teacher, Miss Davenport. Miss Davenport called Carolyn over and asked her to sit with Suzie and "make her feel at home" while she went to greet other children. Carolyn understood Suzie. They became inseparable at school. Every recess, they played hopscotch or climbed the monkey bars or took turns pushing each

other on the swings. They ate together in the cafeteria. Suzie told
Carolyn she lived in Kottinger Village and her daddy was a soldier
in the Army. She had two younger brothers and her mother was
"expecting." Carolyn asked what she was expecting, and Suzie said
a baby brother or sister.

At the end of the year, Suzie said her father had received a
"transfer," and that meant she had to move away. Carolyn's nightmares returned. Only this time, Dock didn't take her away. He
took Suzie.

"Carolyn." She came abruptly awake and found her mother
sitting on the edge of the bed. She brushed the hair back from
Carolyn's forehead. "You're having nightmares again?" When
Carolyn started to cry, her mother patted her leg. Carolyn thought
of Dock and moved away. Mom frowned and folded her hands in
her lap. "I don't know what started them, but you're safe. Everything is fine. Mommy and Daddy are close by."

"Suzie's gone."

"You'll make another friend. You'll see. It won't be as hard next
time."

Carolyn thought it better not to try. First Oma had gone away.
Then Dock. And now Suzie was gone, too.

❄ ❄ ❄

1954

"I'm doing my best, Hildie." Carolyn's father sounded angry and
tired.

"I'm not saying you aren't. Just let me go back to work for a
little while so we can save money for the master bedroom."

"What about the kids?"

"It's partly because of the kids! They can't sleep in the same
room forever, Trip. Besides that, Carolyn was invited to a birthday
party last week, and I couldn't let her go because we couldn't afford
to buy a present. Her first birthday party invitation and I had to
say no."

"It won't kill her."

"Trip . . ."

"You can't just leave them on their own to fend for themselves."

"I can work night shifts. I'd be home by seven in the morning. They wouldn't even know I was gone."

"Remember what happened the last time you took on too much work and didn't get enough rest."

"Yes, Trip." Mommy's voice sharpened. "We still have the hospital bill. It reminds me—*every single month.*"

They lowered their voices, and Carolyn fell asleep again. They argued every night about the same thing until Daddy gave in.

❄   ❄   ❄

1955

Mom's hours changed to "swing shift," and a key was placed under the flowerpot by the front door. "Be sure to put the key back after you unlock the door. Otherwise, it won't be there tomorrow and you'll have to sit outside until Daddy gets home from work. Charlie, if you go anywhere, you be sure to leave a note as to where you're going. Be home by five at the latest. Carolyn, you stay in the house. Play with your doll or read books, but don't go wandering off."

Dad bought a television set. Mom complained about the money. Dad said everyone else in the neighborhood had a television; why shouldn't they?

Carolyn turned it on every day when she came home from school. She felt better hearing voices in the house. She didn't feel as lonely.

"I think it's time you quit working, Hildie. Carolyn needs you."

"She's doing better."

"Better how? Watching TV? Never getting to play outside the house except on weekends? A little girl shouldn't be alone so much. Things could happen."

What things? Carolyn was afraid to ask.

"School lets out in two weeks, Hildemara. What're you going to do then? leave the kids alone *all* day *every* day?"

"I put in for night shift."

"And you think that's going to solve our problems?"

"I don't know, Trip. What will?"

He muttered something and Mom got mad. "I'm trying to help you, and you can't even say a civil word to me! What happened to the man I fell in love with, the one who wanted us to be a *team* and build something *together*? What happened to *him*?"

"The war happened!" Daddy didn't sound mad this time. He said more, but Carolyn couldn't hear. "I've been thinking there might be another way to work this out."

"What way?"

"Take them down to Murietta. . . ."

Carolyn sighed. She fell asleep in her own bed for the first time in months.

5

THE DAY AFTER school let out, Dad put two suitcases in the trunk of the car and drove Carolyn and Charlie down to Oma's farm outside Murietta. Mom cried the night before they left.

Oma had a casserole waiting on the stove and Daddy's favorite angel food cake on a big blue and white willow dish in the middle of the cottage kitchen table. After lunch, Oma told Carolyn and Charlie to play outside while she and Daddy talked. On the way out the door, Carolyn heard Oma say, "They can stay all summer if they want, but I have another proposition to make."

Dad looked less sad when he said he had to leave late in the afternoon. Stooping, he hugged and kissed them both and said things would be better soon. Carolyn couldn't think of anything better than staying with her grandmother.

For the next three weeks, Carolyn and Charlie took turns feeding the chickens and rabbits. Neither Charlie nor Carolyn wanted to

weed the garden, but Oma said they needed to learn how to "pay for
their keep." The quicker they got chores done, the quicker they'd be
free to do whatever they wanted. Charlie always found fun things to
do. They climbed the chinaberry tree and pelted one another with
"bombs." They dug for treasure in the garbage pit, made friends with
the feral cats living in the barn. They weren't quick enough to catch
the mice in the hay, but Charlie managed to capture horned toads,
which he kept in a box until Oma found them and made him turn
them loose. When it got too hot outside, Carolyn sat in the cottage
with Oma, watching *Truth or Consequences, You Bet Your Life* with
Groucho Marx, or *Queen for a Day*.

Mom and Dad came for a Saturday visit. They looked relaxed
and happy. Charlie showed Dad the tree house. He asked Daddy
if they could build one just like it in the walnut tree back home.
Oma gave Carolyn carrots and told her to go feed the rabbits.
Carolyn loved the warm, fuzzy white animals and dawdled while
Mom and Oma sat in the shade of the bay tree. Both rocked in the
aluminum chairs. Oma got up after a while and put her hand on
Mom's shoulder and went inside the cottage. Mom put her head
back and stayed outside. She didn't look happy.

Carolyn went into the small washhouse, where she could hear
Oma and Mommy talking.

"Charlie looks so brown, Mama."

"He's outside as soon as the sun comes up."

"Carolyn is happier than I've seen her in months."

"There are lots of things for her to do here."

"Chores, you mean."

"Chores aren't meant to be punishment, Hildemara. They're
meant to teach responsibility. Chores make you part of the family
enterprise."

Oma and Daddy talked over supper.

"How long do you think it'd take, Trip?"

"Not long if I hired help."

"Could you manage it by the end of summer?"

"No, but no later than Thanksgiving, I think."

When Dad said they had to leave after supper, Charlie asked if he could go home with them. He missed his friends. Dad ruffled his hair. "Not yet, buddy." Charlie missed Mom and Dad more than Carolyn did.

Oma never left them alone. She didn't allow Charlie to "mope around." She took them to the library and checked out adventure stories and picture books. She put out a puzzle of Switzerland and told them stories about her faraway friends Rosie and Solange. When they finished that puzzle, she bought another of an English countryside and told them stories of Daisy Stockhard and fancy afternoon tea parties and daily outings to the royal Kew Gardens. When Carolyn asked if they could have tea parties, too, Oma said of course they could, and they would have one every afternoon if she liked.

Sometimes Oma drove them all the way to Lake Yosemite, where she taught them how to swim. By the middle of summer, Charlie could swim all the way out to the raft, but Carolyn never ventured far from shore. Oma sat under an umbrella and read one of the big books she checked out of the library. On the way home, Oma took them to Wheeler's Truck Stop to have dinner. She told them Mom worked there as a girl and earned tips for being a good waitress to the truckers who carried produce up and down Central Valley Highway 99.

"Your mom is a good, hard worker. You should be very proud of her."

Carolyn could see Oma was.

❄ ❄ ❄

At the end of the summer, Oma drove Carolyn and Charlie home. Something new had been added to the property. A slab of concrete had been poured and walls and roof framed. "I wonder if it's another shed."

Oma laughed. "I hope not!" She parked between the house and the new structure being built.

Neither parent had come home from work yet. Oma took the key from under the flowerpot and unlocked the front door. She pushed it open, but didn't go inside. "You two go unpack. I'm going to take a look at the new project."

Carolyn hurriedly put her playclothes in drawers and her toothpaste, toothbrush, and comb back in the bathroom and raced out to join Oma. Her grandmother stood in the middle of the concrete foundation, between the open two-by-four framed walls. Carolyn came through the open space that would be the front door. Oma pointed. "There's going to be a picture window there and a fireplace over here. Over here is the kitchen with two windows, one looking toward your place and one up the hill." She took Carolyn by the hand. "Accordion doors will cover the washer and dryer, and back here is the bedroom with a nice bathroom, tub, and shower." She smiled as she looked around. "Your daddy does good work."

"Who's going to live here?"

Oma smiled broadly. "Well, who do you think?" She hugged Carolyn against her.

Carolyn felt a surge of relief. "It's like your cottage!"

"Like it, but better. Solid foundation, for one thing. We didn't have the money for one when my cottage was put up. And it's a hundred square feet bigger. There'll be a modern built-in stove and refrigerator in the kitchen, room for a table and three chairs."

A police squad car pulled into the driveway. Charlie came running out of the house and threw himself at Daddy when he got out of the car. Daddy laughed and hugged him, holding him tight and rubbing his knuckles against his hair. "It's about time you came home!" He strode toward the framed cottage. He bent to give Carolyn a quick hug and kiss and then straightened, facing Oma. "So? What do you think?"

"It won't be ready by Thanksgiving." She smiled. "But it takes time to do things right." She looked around again. "And it looks very right to me."

Oma went home to Murietta after breakfast the next morning. She wanted to be home for church the next day. Carolyn climbed an old plum tree near the new cottage. Her folks came out and walked around inside the open structure.

"It won't be like the last time, Hildie. She won't be living under our roof. She'll have her own place."

"I'm just a little uneasy, that's all."

"Uneasy about what?" Daddy sounded annoyed. "I thought everything was settled."

"It is. It's just that Carolyn loves her so much."

"Oh." Daddy stepped closer and put his arms on Mommy's shoulders. "You'll always be her mother, Hildie. Nothing's ever going to change that."

She leaned her head against his shoulder. "If I were a better mother, I'd worry more about her being alone so much than where I'm going to fit in with all the changes we're making. I just want to know there'll be room for me in her life."

"Make room."

"It might already be too late."

❄ ❄ ❄

1956

Carolyn stopped dreaming about Dock when Oma moved into the cottage. No more going into an empty house. She flew off the school bus and raced Charlie up the driveway to Oma's cottage. Her brother always won. Charlie dumped his books by the door, gobbled his cookies, gulped his milk, and rode off on his bike with his redheaded buddy, Mitch Hastings. Carolyn stayed to enjoy "afternoon tea" with Oma. She sipped cream-laced tea and ate triangle-cut egg sandwiches while Oma asked about school. After tea, they went outside together and worked in the garden, weeding the flowers in front and thinning the seedlings in the vegetable garden in back.

When Mom came home, Oma stood on the front steps and called out to her. "Why don't you come over for tea, Hildemara? Rest awhile."

And Mom called back. "Can't today, Mama. I have to get out of this uniform, shower, and change. I'd better get supper started. Maybe tomorrow."

"Tomorrow then. Save some time."

Tomorrow never came, and after a few weeks, Oma stopped asking. She would send Carolyn home when Mom drove in. "Better go do your homework, *Liebling*. And don't forget to help your mother."

But whenever Carolyn offered to help in the kitchen, Mommy would say, "I don't need you, Carolyn. Go and play. Enjoy the sunshine while you can."

After a lonely half hour on the swing, Carolyn went back to Oma's cottage and stayed there until Daddy and Charlie came home.

Oma came over. Carolyn came into the house a minute later and heard her and Mommy arguing. "Why do you chase her outside all the time?"

"I'm not chasing her out."

"What would you call it?"

"I spent most of my childhood inside a house, doing chores. I never had the chance to go out and do whatever I wanted. When she comes to the cottage, you could tell her to play instead of keeping her there."

"I send her home to spend time with her mother, and you just send her right back outside again. . . ."

Carolyn ducked out the door again and ran out to her swing. She saw Oma walking back to the cottage. She looked so sad. Carolyn stayed on the swing until Daddy came home and said she should go in the house and help her mother.

❄ ❄ ❄

Mom took extra shifts at the VA hospital so they could buy more lumber and supplies for building. Daddy finally finished the master bedroom and added a step-down utility porch off the back

of the house, with hookups for a washing machine and dryer. He
bought Mom a mangle for Christmas so she could iron the table-
cloths, sheets, and pillowcases like his mother had. She also ironed
Daddy's shirts, slacks, and boxer shorts and her nurse's uniforms.
The only clothes she didn't iron were the brown polyester pants
and flower-print blouses she wore after work every day.

As soon as Daddy finished the utility porch, he started work on
a larger addition at the front of the house.

Oma came over to take a look around. Daddy proudly laid out
the living room plans: fourteen by twenty feet, twelve-foot wood-
beamed ceiling, skylights, stone fireplace, wall-to-wall carpeting,
and picture windows looking out on the orchard in front. He
showed her the plans he had drawn. "We'll put in a pool with a
patio all around and terrace that back hill, plant a garden, have a
waterfall over there in the corner."

Oma looked as though she had swallowed something that didn't
taste good. "Your own private paradise."

"Something like that."

"Well, it's better than building a bomb shelter like most of the
people in the neighborhood."

"Actually, I was thinking about renting a backhoe to dig one in
the hill. . . ."

The next time Oma invited Mommy over for afternoon tea, she
wouldn't take "Sorry, maybe another time" for an answer.

"I can't stay long. I have to start dinner soon."

"Things won't fall apart if it's not on the table at six on the dot,
Hildemara." Oma sounded irritated. She poured tea in a pretty
pink rose china cup and offered cream and sugar.

Mommy looked at the platter of spicy chicken sandwiches and
egg salad sandwiches with dill and the apple streusel cake. "What is
all this? I didn't forget my birthday, did I?"

"I wanted to treat my daughter to an English afternoon tea, the
kind I used to prepare for Lady Daisy in London."

Mommy gave her an odd smile. "It's lovely. Thank you."

Oma took one seat, Carolyn the other. "If you'd like, we can do this every afternoon when you get home from work. It would be nice, wouldn't it, the three of us sipping tea and taking time to sit and talk awhile?"

"I can't stay more than half an hour."

"If you had a Dutch oven, you could start dinner in the morning before you left for work." Oma sipped her tea. "You'd have an hour to relax when you got home. All you'd have to do is steam some vegetables and set the table. Carolyn could help."

"You always made a four-course dinner, Mama, and dessert, even after you'd worked all day in town. And you walked there and back."

"Until I drove." Oma chuckled as she lifted her teacup. "Papa didn't think much of that idea at first, did he?"

Mom smiled. "We all thought you'd kill yourself in that Model T. You drove like a maniac."

"Probably still do. I felt free. And no one was going to take that away from me." She cut slices of apple streusel and gave Mom a sly smile. "You know, there's no sin in taking advantage of the conveniences available: a car to drive to work, a washer and dryer in the house, an old-fashioned Dutch oven. It buys you time for other things."

"There's always too much to do, Mama. I wish there were more hours in a day."

"And if there were, what would you and Trip do with them?"

Mommy gave a bleak laugh. "Finish building the house."

Carolyn finished a last bite of streusel. Oma cleared away her teacup and saucer and plate. "Why don't you play outside for a while, Carolyn?"

She didn't want to go outside. She wanted to stay inside and listen. "Can I finish the puzzle?"

"I finished it this morning. There's a new one on the coffee table. You can bring it out here and start sorting the pieces, if you like."

Carolyn ran to get the box, dumped the pieces on the table, and began turning them over, sorting colors and searching for edge pieces and corners the way Oma had showed her. Oma and Mommy kept talking.

"You and Trip and the kids ought to take a family vacation."

"There's no money for a vacation."

"There's money for a bomb shelter."

"With the way the world is going right now, a bomb shelter would be more practical than wasting money on a vacation."

"Waste? Let's talk about being practical, shall we? How long would you have to stay inside a bomb shelter before you could come out into the open again, assuming radiation lasts as long as they say it does? I'd rather die in a split second out here in the open and be in heaven in the twinkling of an eye than live underground like a gopher. No sunlight. No garden. Nothing to do. How do you even get fresh air to breathe without letting in the radiation?"

"Everybody's building them."

"People are like lemmings, Hildemara Rose. Yell 'Fire!' and they'll run." They talked about how everyone these days seemed to be worried about spies lurking everywhere, like moles burrowing into the government and science labs, all looking for a way to bring America down. Koreans could brainwash captives and turn them into Manchurian candidates. Russians were spreading Communism all over Eastern Europe. "Everyone is going a little crazy." Oma shook her head in disgust.

"The bomb shelter is Trip's idea, Mama, not mine."

"Plant another idea in his head. I know; I know! The man's only happy when he's working on a project. But I've heard him talk about how he used to hike and camp and fish back in Colorado. Think of the fun you could have with a tent, sleeping bags, and a couple of fishing poles." Oma sipped her tea. "Charlie is thirteen already. He's always off somewhere with his friends. In another six years, he'll go away to college. And Carolyn's going to be nine soon." Oma lowered her voice. "She needs her mother."

"Like I needed you, Mama?" A quiet edge of bitterness crept into her mother's voice.

"Yes. And where was I? Working, always working. If anyone

has a right to talk about this, I do!" Oma turned the teacup in its saucer. "Just so you know, I came up here to tear down walls, not help you build them."

Mom fidgeted. "I don't know what to make of this."

"Make of what?"

"Sitting in your kitchen, having tea."

Oma scowled at her. "I've invited you over every day for weeks. You wouldn't come!"

"I've spent most of my life trying to live up to your standards and failing."

"So you're going to punish me in my old age. Is that it?"

"I still don't come up to your standards, do I? I'm not a good mother. Trip's too busy to be a father. There's no pleasing you."

"Now, you listen to me, Hildemara Rose. And you listen good. You never failed me, not once. Nor did I fail you, if it comes to that. You were small and sickly when you were born. Was that your fault? You had the most to overcome. I was afraid you wouldn't even survive that first winter out there in the frozen wheat fields. I almost lost you again when you had pneumonia. Do you remember? And I could still lose you if you keep on as you are. Yes! I was harder on you than the others. I wanted you to grow up strong so no one would be able to hold you down. So I pushed you. I pushed hard. And, thank God, you pushed back. Now look at you."

"You sound proud." Mom sounded surprised.

"I am." She raised her teacup and smiled. "I'm proud of both of us."

6

AFTER SEVERAL HEATED discussions muffled by the master bedroom door, Dad threw away his plans for the bomb shelter and bought an Airstream trailer instead. One weekend a month, Mom and Dad packed the trailer and took off with Carolyn and Charlie in the backseat of the sedan. Carolyn found herself looking forward to the weekends away, even though Oma never went along. "Someone has to feed Bullet and pick up the mail." She would wave as they drove away. "Bring me back a souvenir!"

Pigeon Point was Carolyn's favorite place. Dad parked the trailer on the strip of land north of the lighthouse. They set up camp and ate Chef Boyardee spaghetti, sweet corn, and white bread with butter and jam off paper plates. After dinner, they played Chinese checkers, Scrabble, or hearts. When it was bedtime, Mom folded the table down, and the booth seats made a double bed for Carolyn and Charlie. Carolyn liked having Charlie, Mom, and Dad close by. She loved the sound of the foghorn going off every few minutes and surf crashing against the rocks within a few hundred feet of the trailer.

While Charlie and Dad caught Capistrano, blue moon, and shiner perch in the churning white foam pools, Mom and Carolyn climbed down the steep path to the cove beach on the other side of the lighthouse. They combed the beach for seashells and pretty, curling, polished bits of driftwood. Sometimes Carolyn put her arms out, wishing she could ride the wind like the seagulls overhead. She followed the waves down and ran back as they rolled toward her while Mom lounged in the sunshine.

Once they drove north across the Golden Gate and headed west for Dillon Beach near Tomales Bay. All four went out at low tide to dig gooey-neck clams. Carolyn's arms weren't long enough to reach down into the holes she dug, but Charlie managed with his gangling limbs to bring one up in triumph. When the feast was laid on the table, Carolyn fled out the door and threw up in the bushes.

Another time, Dad drove for hours until he found Salt Point. The next morning, Mom, Charlie, and Carolyn watched Dad plod around in the deep tidal pools wearing chest-high rubber waders, prying abalone off the rocks. It was up to Mom to cut the sea snails from their shells and use a mallet to soften the muscle. Dad laughed and said it was a good way for Mom to vent her frustrations. Abalone tasted better than tough, sand-gritty gooey-neck clams. And Carolyn loved the lustrous, iridescent shells. Dad hung them around the front entry of the house. Oma used one as a soap dish.

Mom and Dad decided to take the summer off from building. Instead, they packed for a trip and hooked up the trailer. After three long days of travel over deserts and mountains, Carolyn finally met Grandpa Otis and Grandma Marg in Colorado Springs.

Grandpa Otis lifted her onto his lap. "Look at this pretty little honeybee."

When Carolyn struggled to get away from him, Dad grabbed her by the arm and hauled her out into the backyard. He shook her hard and asked what in the blazes was the matter with her. How could she hurt her grandfather like that? He told her she'd better be nice or she'd be sorry. Mom came out, too, and told him to stop it.

Grandpa didn't touch her again. Neither did Dad. They sat in the small living room talking in low voices. Grandma gave her two cookies and a glass of milk, but she wasn't hungry or thirsty. Grandma and Mom sat at the table with her, talking like nothing had happened. Charlie went outside to play.

It took three days for Carolyn to feel comfortable enough to sit beside Grandpa on the sofa. He read Bible stories to her. After a while, she relaxed against him. He didn't smell anything like Dock. His heart didn't beat as fast. His breathing was easy and relaxed. She liked the sound of his deep voice. She closed her eyes for a while and heard a click. She opened her eyes to see Mom smile and set a camera on the side table.

The next morning they left, heading south this time to Mesa Verde, with its steep, narrow paths and cliff ruins, and on to Monument Valley, with its familiar buttes. Charlie recognized scenes from Westerns and talked about marauding Indians who scalped people and tied them down on top of red ant hills. Mom looked back at Carolyn and told Charlie to talk about cavalry rescues instead.

They spent one whole day at the Grand Canyon. They drove to Bryce the next, taking a hike through the hoodoos before settling into the trailer for dinner and a good night's sleep. "We'll only have time to drive through Zion," Dad told Mom while they lay in bed a few feet away. "Then we'll have to head for Death Valley."

They spent the last night at Furnace Creek, sleeping in pools of their own sweat. Up at dawn, they made the long drive over the Sierras to the Central Valley, where the scents of sandy soil, almond orchards, and alfalfa fields reminded Carolyn of Oma's farm.

As soon as they pulled into the driveway, Carolyn wanted to jump out and run to the cottage. Dad told her to help unpack the trailer. Mom told her to dump her dirty clothes in the laundry room. Then, finally, "Okay, you can go." Unleashed, Carolyn ran.

Oma met her on the front porch, arms open, and hugged her tight. "It's about time you got home. It's been lonely around here." Oma lifted Carolyn's face and kissed her on both cheeks. All the

postcards Carolyn had sent were taped to the front of Oma's refrigerator. Seeing how much Oma had missed her, Carolyn offered to
stay home with Oma next time.

"Oh no, you won't. There's a whole world out there to see, and
your mother and father are showing you a corner of it. Where
would I be right now if I stayed home because I was afraid my
mother might miss me?" She waved Carolyn to a seat at the
kitchen table and turned the burner on under her teakettle. "So
how was it? Did you like your other grandparents?"

"They were nice." Carolyn didn't tell her how she'd hurt
Grandpa Otis's feelings or made Daddy mad, how she'd run away
and hidden for hours, worrying everyone. And she didn't tell her
how Mom complained when Dad would only stop for gas or a
quick lunch before driving again. Oma didn't like complaining.

Oma folded her hands on the table. "Tell me what you saw."

"It's all there on your refrigerator."

"Well, you must have seen other things along the way," Oma
pressed.

Not really. Dad had driven from dawn to dusk, hour after hour,
while she and Charlie half dozed in the backseat. They'd both seen
places they wanted to stop, but Dad said they didn't have time. He
told them they could play when they got to the campground, but
then when they did, it was near dusk, time to eat, time to shower,
time to get ready for bed. Dad was "dog-tired" and didn't feel like
playing games. He'd been driving all day. Carolyn shrugged. What
did Oma want her to say?

"Well. Now that you're all home, I can make a trip to the farm
and see Hitch and Donna Martin about business."

"Can I come with you?"

"I thought you didn't like traveling!"

Traveling with Oma wasn't the same as traveling with Dad and
Mom. "Please?"

"You'll have to ask your parents."

They didn't see any reason why she shouldn't. Charlie would
be off all day on his bicycle or at the high school pool. Dad had to

work. Mom did, too. It seemed no one would miss her. In fact, it would be easier for everyone if she went with Oma. Mom washed Carolyn's clothes and repacked some in a small duffel bag. They walked over together in the morning.

"How long will you be gone, Mama?"

"I was thinking it might be time to see Bernhard and Elizabeth. Carolyn hardly knows her cousin Eddie. And I haven't been down to Clotilde's in two years. She has an apartment in Hollywood. That would take a couple of days' driving time. A week, ten days? If that's all right with you."

Mom bit her lip and looked down at Carolyn. "I guess it's okay."

"We'll call you, Hildemara."

"Take good care of her."

"You know I will." Carolyn and Oma answered at the same time.

Mom looked sort of sad. "Well, you two have a good time together." Turning away, she lifted her hand in good-bye and headed back to the house.

❊ ❊ ❊

Traveling with Oma turned out to be even more fun than Carolyn expected. Oma drove fast with the windows all rolled down. She stopped twice before they even reached the outskirts of Tracy. "I've got to stretch these old legs."

When they arrived at Uncle Bernhard's nursery south of Sacramento, he took them on a tour through the rows of fruit trees in five-gallon buckets, Cousin Eddie trailing along behind. He stood a foot taller than Carolyn and had more muscle than Charlie. Aunt Elizabeth made fried chicken, mashed potatoes, and steamed corn for dinner. They had an extra bedroom for Oma and Carolyn to share.

The next morning, Oma said it was time to be off to Murietta. Everyone hugged and kissed. "Don't make it so long between visits,

Mama. Any chance you could get Hildie and Trip over here? We haven't seen them in a couple of years. Charlie's probably half-grown by now."

"They're building."

Uncle Bernie laughed. "Well, we know all about that."

❋ ❋ ❋

After a couple of days at the farm, where Oma talked business with Hitch and Donna Martin, they drove to Hollywood to visit Aunt Clotilde. She was tall and thin and dressed in narrow black pants and a bulky white sweater. She talked fast and laughed a lot. She took Carolyn and Oma to the movie studio where she worked in the costume department. Garments lined the walls, and sewing machines whirred as half a dozen people sat bent over pieces of fabric. Clotilde gaily called for everyone's attention and introduced Oma and Carolyn. "Okay, folks. Back to work." She laughed. "You have to see the back lot, Mama. It's fantastic!" She led Oma and Carolyn out. She knew everyone: makeup artists, set designers, directors, gaffers and grips, and even a few movie stars who, out of makeup and costume, looked like ordinary people.

One man looked Carolyn over with interest. "I didn't know you had such a pretty niece, Cloe."

"I didn't either!" Aunt Clotilde grinned and draped her arm around Carolyn's shoulders. "She's grown up since the last time I saw her. I've been asking my mother how my plain-Jane sister could come by such a pretty, willowy, blue-eyed little blonde."

Oma grunted. "Hildemara is pretty enough."

"Oh, Mama. I didn't mean anything by it. You know how much I love Hildie, but look at Carolyn. She's pretty enough to be in the movies."

Oma and Clotilde talked far into the night, quiet murmurs. In the morning, the three of them shared yogurt and fresh fruit for breakfast. Clotilde hugged and kissed Oma good-bye. "Come back again soon, Mama." Oma promised she would. Aunt Clotilde brushed Carolyn's cheek with her fingers and smiled. Leaning down, she kissed her on the cheek. "Give your mother my love. She's very special. Just like you." Pulling her robe more fully around herself, she crossed her arms and stood at the door as they left.

Oma didn't head north. "Since we've come all the way down here to Hollywood, we might as well go a little farther and see Disneyland."

Carolyn couldn't believe her good luck. "Charlie is going to be so mad he didn't come along."

"We're not going to say anything about it. It's not like I planned it. We don't want him feeling left out."

They checked into a hotel next to an orange grove and arrived at the gates of Disneyland as they opened the next morning. "We're going to beat the crowd to the train ride."

After they'd taken the grand circle tour, her grandmother took her hand and pulled her along, another destination already set in her mind. When Carolyn saw what it was, she gulped. "A rocket!"

"We're going. It's the closest we'll ever get to the moon." Caught up in Oma's excitement, Carolyn lost her fear and began to enjoy herself. Later, Oma took her on the riverboat ride, then to a race-track, and even a stagecoach. They saw a movie called *A Tour of the West* at the Circarama theater and an exhibit based on one of Oma's favorite books, *20,000 Leagues Under the Sea*.

That night, Oma gave her fair warning before calling Mom and Dad. "Not a word about Disneyland. We don't want to hurt anyone's feelings." But Mom didn't even ask to talk to Carolyn. Oma talked about Aunt Clotilde and the costume workroom and the back lot. "We're on our way home. I'm driving up the coast. The Central Valley is too hot. Two days, I think, maybe three."

On the drive north, Oma talked about the author John Steinbeck and the story he'd written about the Okies who had left the dust bowl and come west to California's Central Valley. "Good, hard-working people like the Martins. I'm blessed to have them. You should read *The Grapes of Wrath* when you're older. Find out what times were like when your mother was growing up in Murietta."

❄ ❄ ❄

They arrived home in time for dinner. Charlie bragged about spending every day of the last week at the Alameda County Fair with his best friend, Mitch Hastings. Oma winked at Carolyn and talked about Uncle Bernie, Aunt Elizabeth, and Aunt Clotilde.

Charlie tapped on Carolyn's bedroom door after Mom and Dad went to bed. "I didn't mean to rub it in about the fair." He flopped down beside her and explained how Mom had given him money for admission and meals. "She dropped me off every morning on her way to work." He stayed until Dad or Mitch's father picked them up just before closing. "It got pretty boring after the first couple days." He gave her a sly grin. "Can you keep a secret?"

Carolyn knew all about keeping secrets.

"Mitch and I snuck into the grandstands and watched the horse races." They'd made friends with a jockey while hanging around the stables. "He broke the rules and let Mitch ride his horse. I didn't have the guts." Charlie and Mitch had shared a pilfered beer and gone on the carnival rides with a couple of girls they picked up. "So, what'd you and Oma do?"

"Went to Uncle Bernie and Aunt Elizabeth's."

"How's Eddie?"

"Bigger."

"I thought you were going to the farm."

"We did. Then we went down to see Aunt Clotilde."

"See any movie stars?"

Nobody she recognized. She didn't mention that Aunt Clotilde said she was pretty enough to be in movies, or Disneyland, or any of the other stops up the coast of California.

"Boy, am I glad I stayed home." Charlie stretched. "I'm sorry you missed the fair."

Carolyn couldn't imagine anything worse than being dropped off in the morning and spending twelve to fourteen hours wandering alone among crowds of strangers.

1961

The summer before Carolyn entered high school brought back nightmares she never thought to have again. Mom and Dad focused on Charlie, who had only one year left before he'd launch into the wild blue yonder of college, hopefully on an academic or football scholarship. Oma mounted her own campaign for Carolyn to think about college, too. Why shouldn't a girl have the same opportunities her brother did? Her mother had gone to nurses' training, hadn't she?

Carolyn spent the summer alone. Sometimes Mitch Hastings came by to ask her brother if he wanted to do something. She hardly saw Charlie. He had a summer job at Kohl's Furniture Store. Even when he was home, they hardly talked. He'd eat and take off with Mitch. They'd go to the movies or the Gay 90s. At the end of the summer, Mitch came over on a motorcycle and took Charlie for a ride. Charlie talked about the motorcycle at dinner that night. He wanted one, too, and figured he could afford to buy one with what he'd saved from his summer job. Dad told him to hold off and think a little more about it. Mom said Charlie would need that money for school.

A week later, Dad tossed Charlie keys to a 1959 red Chevy Impala. "You get a ticket and that little baby will be parked for a month."

Charlie whooped. "No more riding the bus!"

Charlie gave Carolyn a ride on her first day of high school. He told her to stay clear of the upperclass lawn. "They're looking for fresh meat, and you're cute. Mitch thinks so, too." He grinned.

Carolyn felt a fluttering sensation in the pit of her stomach. "Does he?"

When they pulled into the student lot, boys swarmed the car. "Whoa, Charlie! Where'd you get this baby? She's a beaut." One boy opened the hood.

Another opened Carolyn's door. "Hey, Charlie! Who's this?"

Charlie got out of the car. "This is my little sister, Carolyn, and keep your grubby hands off. Carolyn, meet the zoo." He rattled off a dozen names. Some she had seen at the house. Most were complete strangers. Charlie came around the car. "She's shy. Okay? Come on, Sis. They don't bite."

One of the bigger boys grinned broadly. "I'd like to."

"Shut up, Brady."

Even close to Charlie, Carolyn felt hemmed in, trapped. Were all high school boys this big and bold?

A motorcycle roared into the lot and pulled in a few feet away. Mitch took off his helmet, swung his leg over the bike, and watched the gathering. "Hey, Mitch!" Charlie headed for his best friend. Carolyn's heart jumped. When Mitch said hi to her, she couldn't speak, her mouth went so dry. She looked down when her face heated up. When they all headed for the main building, she followed. Carolyn noticed Charlie couldn't walk more than a few feet without someone saying hi and asking how was his summer vacation, what'd he do. She felt conspicuous and uncomfortable. She wished she'd taken the bus.

When two girls came over to Charlie, he forgot about her. Mitch stepped into the main office and came out with a school map. He pointed out where they were on the map. Checking her class list, he gave her directions. Map and class schedule in hand, Carolyn found her way around. At lunch break, she sat at a table with other nervous freshman girls. When Charlie and Mitch came over, the girls gawked and fell silent. Mitch ignored them, but Charlie grinned at them all before turning to Carolyn. "I've got football practice after school. You'll have to take the bus home."

The girls whispered as they watched Charlie and Mitch walk away. Carolyn knew before lunch hour ended which girls wanted to be friends with her because Charlie was tall and handsome and he played football.

To please Oma, Carolyn focused on getting good grades right from the beginning of freshman year. She met other studious girls who didn't socialize with the in-crowd. A few of Charlie's friends tried to make conversation with her in the school corridors. She didn't encourage them, and they moved on to others who liked to flirt. Carolyn watched boys and girls pair up. Charlie put out the word his sister was off-limits, which was fine with her. She felt uncomfortable in her own skin when a boy looked at her, especially one she admired, like Mitch Hastings.

❄   ❄   ❄

1962

By the time spring rolled around, Carolyn got her wish. No one noticed her. She felt invisible as she moved through the thronged corridors. The only boy who said hi every time he saw her was Mitch. Midterm he transferred into her study hall and sat in the front row. A linebacker, Mitch was taller and broader than Charlie, certainly too big for the student desks. He moved to the back row the next day, taking an empty desk across from her.

Sometimes, she felt him staring at her, but when she glanced his way, he'd be scribbling notes and flipping through his textbook.

She knew from Charlie he didn't date many girls, especially ones who "went after him."

Mom and Dad spent most of Carolyn's freshman year asking Charlie what he planned to do after he graduated. Charlie didn't know. Mom and Dad became increasingly frustrated. "You're a senior! You can't put off sending out applications for college!" The tension mounted. It got so Carolyn wished she could live with Oma. The more Dad and Mom pressured Charlie, the more Charlie dug in his heels.

Charlie vented to Carolyn. "I wish they'd get off my back. Take a wild guess what they did."

"What?"

"Called Mrs. Vardon. Now I've got the college counselor breathing down my neck. She pulled me out of study hall yesterday." He had to report to her office every day until he finished filling out a stack of college applications, wrote essays, and gathered and made copies of recommendation letters from teachers, coaches, and his part-time employer. "Guess which university sat on top of the pile. Berkeley!"

"What have you got against Berkeley?"

"Nothing, except I'm not that impressed with their football program." He gave her a conspiratorial grin. "Don't tell anyone, but I've applied to USC." He'd already talked to the college coach and been assured he qualified for a football scholarship.

"I'm not telling them anything until I graduate. Let 'em sweat!" He grinned with defiant pleasure. "I can hardly wait to see Dad's face when I tell him I'm going to play for the Trojans."

Charlie followed through with his plans, but Carolyn could tell he felt rather let down when Dad gave his blessing. And his instincts about the football program proved true, when USC went to the Rose Bowl during his first year.

Oma said she'd never seen the Tournament of Roses Parade and this would be a good time to go since Charlie was on the USC team in the big game. "Why don't you try to get time off, Hildemara?"

"Don't you think I'd like to go? Every day I miss is a day off our vacation time."

"Do you mind if I take Carolyn?"

Mom's face tightened, and then her shoulders drooped. "It'd mean a lot to Charlie to have family at the game."

Dad said he couldn't take time off either, so Oma took Carolyn. They stood among the crowds along Pasadena's Colorado Boulevard, watching gorgeous flower-scented floats, marching bands, and horseback riders pass by. Later, they attended the big game, where they could barely spot Charlie among the other Trojan uniformed players "warming the bench." He'd been happy to make the team, and he said he'd help win it again next year. They spent the night at Aunt Cloe's Beverly Hills mansion. Her producer husband was on-set somewhere in England, and her step-children off at boarding schools.

❄ ❄ ❄

1963

About the time Carolyn started eleventh grade, Dock came back in her dreams. Sometimes she awoke aroused and confused. Guilt and shame caught her by the throat. She knew the facts of life. She'd taken biology. She'd overheard whispered conversations about sex in the girls' locker room. Girls who "did it" were considered sluts.

What would people say if they knew she'd lost her virginity while playing games with the man who lived next door? She'd only been in kindergarten, but it didn't do any good to tell herself it wasn't her fault. She knew it was. She had gone over there day after day, hadn't she? She'd told Dock she loved him. She let him do what he wanted.

Carolyn went to church with her parents—and Oma, when she wasn't away on one of her trips. She knew God existed. She imagined Him as old, with a long white beard and dressed in long white robes, His eyes blazing, and ready to cast the damned into a lake of fire. Was that where she would end up? God knew everything, didn't He? He saw everything. God would know she boiled inside. He probably knew why, even if she didn't.

She listened to Rev. Elias talk about the peace of God and doing what was right. She needed desperately to talk to someone. When she went over to talk with Oma, she found her grandmother packing for another trip. Oma spent more time away than at the cottage. She went to visit Uncle Bernie and Aunt Elizabeth or Aunt Clotilde. She flew to New York to see Aunt Rikka when her paintings were shown in some famous gallery. This time she was going to spend a week in San Francisco with her old friend Hedda Herkner, whose husband had died of a heart attack. Oma smiled over her shoulder as she folded a dress into her suitcase. "You're all grown-up, Carolyn. You don't need me."

❋ ❋ ❋

Two days after Oma left for San Francisco, a student came into Carolyn's civics class and gave the teacher a message. Mrs. Schaffer burst into tears when she read it. "President Kennedy has been shot down in Dallas, Texas."

Everyone sat stunned for a few seconds and then started asking questions.

A few girls burst into tears. Even a few boys looked ready to cry, though they tried hard not to show it. Mrs. Schaffer said everyone was to go to the auditorium for a school assembly. The principal would tell them everything he knew.

The principal cried, too.

Carolyn felt hollow and numb inside. Shouldn't she be scared? Others were. Shouldn't she be angry? Others were. She heard the news and waited to feel something, *anything*.

The assembly ended after less than fifteen minutes. School was dismissed. Parents would know about it. Students with cars headed for the parking lot. Most headed for the buses lined up in front of the high school. Someone had already lowered the American flag to half-mast. Carolyn got on her bus and sat in the back row. She stared out the window while others talked, sobbed, cussed in whispers, made speculations about the future. What would Kennedy's death mean to America? Would the space program end? What about the Peace Corps? So much for those who dreamed of being astronauts or going to foreign countries and solving world problems. So much for hoping the world would ever get any better.

One by one, students got off at their stops. As the rows of seats emptied, Carolyn moved forward row by row until she sat near the front. She could see the bus driver's face in the rearview mirror. Tears ran down his cheeks. She stepped forward and clung to the pole next to the steps. "This is my stop, Mr. Landers." She had the feeling he would have forgotten if she hadn't spoken. He pulled over, stopped, and opened the bus doors.

Carolyn walked up the long driveway. The birds still sang. Everything still looked the same. She wished Oma were home, so she wouldn't have to go into an empty house. She took the key out from under the flowerpot and unlocked the door. The place felt like a tomb—closed up, airless, silent.

Craving the sound of a human voice, she turned on the television. Every channel covered the assassination. She saw the joyful scenes before the shooting—people holding up welcome signs, others watching from windows and rooftops, the smiling president and his pretty wife waving from the car. Then three shots. A Secret Service man getting out of the car behind the president. People in the crowd screamed and cried; policemen looked up to see where the shots had come from. Shaking, she wanted to scream. She wanted to put her foot through the television. Instead, she shut it off and went into the kitchen.

Mom had filled the cookie jar with Oreos. Leftovers filled the refrigerator. A roast defrosted on the counter, blood pooling in the plastic wrap. Carolyn pictured Jackie with her husband's blood on her designer suit.

She went over to the cottage, wandered through Oma's flower garden, and then took the key from under the mat and opened the door. The cottage felt like an empty shell without Oma, even with sunlight coming through the windows. But it smelled familiar and felt cozy. She went to the bedroom and crawled under the covers of Oma's bed, wishing she could curl up against Oma as she'd done when she was a little girl. It was the only time she could remember feeling truly safe as a child.

Only a moment seemed to pass, and she heard someone call her name. She heard a door open.

"Carolyn." Mom's voice came closer, voice hoarse with worry. "Carolyn!" Carolyn felt someone shaking her. "We've been looking all over for you!"

"I'm here," Carolyn mumbled, mouth dry. Her head felt strange. What was she doing in Oma's bed? Then she remembered. The president had been shot. Despair engulfed her.

"Didn't you hear us calling?"

"I didn't hear anything." She felt sick. "I don't want to hear anything."

"Come on home, Carolyn." She pulled the covers down. "You can sleep in your own room." She stood in the doorway. "Be sure to make the bed before you come."

Inexplicably angry, Carolyn yanked the covers up again. "I'm not coming! I'm sleeping here tonight!"

Mom sat on the edge of the bed. "Carolyn, we're all upset. . . ."

Carolyn shifted away. "Dad will have the television on. He'll want to watch the news over and over again. You know he will. And you'll be mangling something." She started to cry. "I don't want to see Kennedy shot again and again. I don't want to keep hearing about it!" She covered her head with the blankets. "Just go away, Mom. Please. Just let me go to sleep and pretend it never happened."

Mom rubbed her back and sighed heavily. "You're not the only one who feels that way." She stood. "Are you sure you're okay here alone?"

Carolyn wanted to scream at her. Of course she wasn't okay. She had never been okay. What kind of a mother would leave her vulnerable little girl alone every afternoon? A mother who didn't care, that's what kind. Why should her mother care now?

No one was ever home when she got there. What difference did it make if she spent the night in the cottage—or anywhere else, for that matter? It wasn't like Dock would come back after more than ten years. Even he hadn't wanted her in the end. "I'm fine, Mom. Go away."

"Well, if you're sure . . ." Her mother sounded hesitant. Something in her voice caught Carolyn's attention. She pulled the blankets off her head, but her mother was already heading for the door. As it closed behind her, Carolyn wept. She lay in the darkness, wishing her mother had argued a little. She wished she'd sat on the bed for a few minutes longer.

But then, she'd have to care to do that.

8

1965

While everyone else in her class grew more excited with the approach of graduation, Carolyn dreaded it. It meant she would have to leave home. She didn't have any great desire to go to college, but it seemed to be what everyone expected of her.

Oma made calls and fanned out university and state college brochures and application forms on the kitchen table. "War or not, the world goes on, Carolyn, and you have to make plans." UC Berkeley was close. She could come home on weekends. So she applied there, for Oma's sake, as well as Chabot junior college and Heald College in Hayward.

Dad seemed stunned when Carolyn was accepted at Berkeley. Oma asked why, for goodness' sake. "Did you think your daughter was stupid?"

Her brother came home for her graduation. It passed in a blur. Dad took pictures. Mom made a nice dinner. Oma decorated a cake. Carolyn received cards of congratulations and money from Uncle Bernie and Aunt Elizabeth, Aunt Clotilde, and Aunt Rikka.

Charlie grew restless. He wanted to go into town and see friends, although most of them had gone elsewhere for the summer. Dad asked if he ever heard from Mitch Hastings. Charlie said they talked. Mitch's mom had died of cancer, and his dad had moved to Florida and remarried. Mitch had made the Ohio State team, second-string. Mitch wouldn't be coming back to Paxtown anytime soon, if ever.

Carolyn felt a pang of disappointment. She supposed it was silly to wish Mitch Hastings might come home someday and see her as someone other than Charlie's kid sister.

"What do you say we take a ride, Sis?"

Mom told them to go ahead and have some fun.

They drove into town. Charlie said he was proud of her. She had received an award for being on the honor roll every semester since freshman year. "Why so glum?"

"Just scared, I guess."

"Scared of what?"

"Whether I can make it or not."

"You'll make it." Charlie drove from the high school to the end of Main Street, turned around, and came back. He honked and waved at people he knew. Everyone remembered her brother. He talked about college friends and professors, classes and football games, beer busts and pretty sorority girls. Charlie, so full of confidence, afraid of nothing.

"I'm amazed Dad agreed to send you to Berkeley. It's a hotbed of subversives!"

"He was always after you to go."

"Yeah, well, you're another story. It doesn't seem like a good fit for you. USC is hard enough, even for a coddled football player. But Berkeley! Man, that place has a reputation for chewing people up and spitting them out."

"Oma talked me into it."

He laughed. "You're going to like living in another universe, Carolyn." He honked at someone else and waved before giving her a quick glance. "Just don't turn into a hippy."

"You're the one letting your hair grow." Dad had made more than one comment about it over the last few days. "How do you get away with it? I thought you had to keep it short for football."

Charlie scowled. He didn't answer immediately. "Football's something else that chews you up and spits you out. Seems like a stupid waste of time when you consider all the guys going to Vietnam and dying to protect our freedom."

Her body tightened. She stared at him. He gave her a quick glance, an odd look on his face. "Mitch joined the Marine Corps. Did I tell you that?"

Her heart sank. "You said he was playing football for Ohio State."

"He was. He quit."

Her heart started pounding. She kept looking at Charlie. "I hope the war ends before you finish college."

"It won't." He stared straight ahead. Someone honked. He didn't notice this time.

"I hope you don't get drafted."

"I won't get drafted, Carolyn."

She clenched her hands at the assurance in his tone. "Don't enlist, Charlie. Please, don't even think about enlisting."

"I already did."

She put her hands over her ears. "No, you didn't! Don't tell me you did! Don't!"

Charlie turned off at the end of Main Street and took the road past the fairgrounds, out to the road along the hills. "Take it easy."

Take it easy? Take it easy! She couldn't catch her breath.

"Someone has to go. Why not me? Why is it always someone else who has to do the dirty work? You're going to have to help me break the news to Mom and Dad."

When she tried to open the car door, he yanked her back. "What are you doing? Are you crazy?" Swerving to the side of the road, Charlie slammed on the brakes. "Are you trying to get us both killed?"

"You're the one who's going to get killed!" Sobbing, she jerked herself free, scrambled out of the car, and ran.

Charlie caught up with her. "Carolyn!" He pulled her around and locked his arms around her. "Hey. I didn't think you'd take it like this."

She felt half-smothered against his USC jacket. She clung to it, burying her face in his chest. "I don't want you to go, Charlie. Don't go. Please don't go."

"It's too late to change my mind, even if I wanted to, which I don't."

She hadn't heard the worst of it yet.

❉ ❉ ❉

"The Marine Corps?" Dad turned ghastly white. *"The Marine Corps?"*

Charlie looked confident. "Why not be among the best of the best?"

"Why did you do it?" Dad swore. "Because Mitch Hastings joined up?"

"No, Dad. I can think for myself. I'm doing it to serve my country." He sounded angry. "I thought you, of all people, would understand." He looked from Dad to Mom and gave a nervous laugh. "You raised me to be a patriot, didn't you? You've been talking about what it means to be an American for as long as I can remember. *You* served. Why shouldn't I?"

"I was a medic, Charlie! We went in after the damage was done, to clean up the mess. The Marines are always the *first* in, the *first* up the beach!" His voice broke.

Mom covered her face and wept.

Charlie looked embarrassed. "I'll be okay."

"Yeah. Every young man thinks he's going to be okay. You signed up to be cannon fodder!" Dad shoved his chair back and left the table. Mom looked at Charlie, tried to speak. Nothing came out.

"I'm doing the right thing, Mom."

Her mouth trembled. "It's not a football game, Charlie."

Charlie's face tightened. "Do you think I don't know that?"

"Why didn't you discuss this with us first?"

"I don't need your permission. It's my life. It's my decision." His defiance melted when Mom started to cry again. "Mom . . ." He reached out to her. She got up and headed for the bedroom.

Charlie pushed his chair back and gave Carolyn an apologetic look. "I've got to get out of here." He glanced toward the back of the house. "I wish they'd stop thinking of me as their little boy."

"Can I go with you?"

"Not this time. Okay? I'm supposed to meet a couple of the guys at the Gay 90s."

Carolyn sat at the table alone, listening to Charlie's red Impala speed down the gravel driveway. She wished she could run, too. She wished she could take off and go hang out with friends who would understand what she was feeling, maybe help her make some kind of sense out of the world.

She went to the cottage. Oma turned off the television and patted the space beside her on the sofa.

"Charlie's enlisted in the Marine Corps."

Oma let out a deep breath. "I knew he'd done something. He looked different."

Carolyn put her head in Oma's lap and wept. "I don't want him to go."

Oma stroked her hair. "It's not your choice, *Liebling*. All you can do is live your life and let Charlie live his." She rested her hand on Carolyn's head. "It's a lesson I've had to learn over the years."

"I'm going to worry about him every day."

"No. You're going to go to the university and study and meet interesting people. You're going to make dreams for yourself. You'll be so busy you won't have time to fret."

"They'll send him to Vietnam."

"We don't know that yet."

"They will, Oma."

"Then we'll pray. We'll get everyone in the church and all our relatives and friends praying, too. And we'll write letters to him so he knows we love him. Sometimes that's all you can do, Carolyn.

Love people for who they are, pray, and leave them in God's hands."

Carolyn wasn't sure she could trust God. After all, God hadn't done anything to protect her from Dock.

Carolyn worked all summer serving hamburgers and milk shakes at the local diner, and Charlie came in every day. He didn't have to report to San Diego for basic training until the end of summer. Mitch had already finished basic and transferred to infantry training. Charlie drove down when Mitch called and said he had weekend liberty. When Charlie came home, he disappeared for a day without saying where he was going. He came into the diner just before Carolyn finished work and gave her a ride home.

"I decided not to wait. I'm flying to San Diego on Friday. I'll be in basic by the beginning of next week."

She made fists in her lap and looked out the window. "Why are you in such a hurry to die, Charlie?"

"I don't plan to die. I just can't stand hanging around here any longer listening to Mom cry or having Dad sit and stare at the news. It's better if I go. You want to be the one to drive me to the airport?"

"No."

"Come on, Sis." He tried to coax her. "I'll loan you my car for four years."

"I don't want your car." She wanted to know her brother would be safe, and he'd just obliterated that hope.

He sighed dramatically. "I guess I'll take the bus and then a cab." She knew he expected her to give in.

Dad drove Charlie to the airport. Mom closed herself in the master bedroom and didn't come out all that day or that evening.

Three weeks later, Carolyn packed and tried to prepare herself to leave home.

Dad said Mom wasn't up to taking her, and he had to work. Her grandmother would make sure she got settled.

❄ ❄ ❄

Carolyn carried her things into the dorm. When everything had been put away in her small room, Oma suggested they go for a walk. "I'd like to see the campus before I leave." They wandered for two hours along the walkways past great halls and through plazas. Oma wanted to see Sather Gate, the Bancroft Library, and the Campanile. "I would've given anything to attend a university like this. My father took me out of school when I turned twelve. He thought education was wasted on a girl."

"You know more than most of the teachers I've met, Oma."

Oma gave a short, humorless laugh. "You don't give up just because someone says you can't do something. Sometimes telling someone she can't makes her want it all the more."

Oma took Carolyn's hand as they walked back to the old gray Plymouth. "Time for me to go." Oma hugged her tightly and patted her cheek. "You'll be learning from masters. Take advantage of every moment you have."

"I'll do my best."

"Your best is all anyone can ask."

❄ ❄ ❄

Carolyn kept her word. She attended every class, took voluminous notes, studied late into the night, turned in all her assignments on time, and passed her midterms.

Charlie made it through basic and came home on leave. He drove to Berkeley and took Carolyn over to San Francisco for a day. He'd changed since she'd last seen him. He didn't say much about training, but pressed her for information about her classes, how she liked Berkeley, if she was finding her way okay. She said everything was fine, just fine.

They sat on a bench along Fisherman's Wharf. Girls looked at Charlie as they walked by. He looked back at a few. She teased him. "Wishing your little sister wasn't here?"

He laughed and said being locked up in a barracks for weeks on end tended to make a man appreciate the scenery more. "What about you, Sis? Having any fun?"

"Fun? I'm concentrating on keeping my head above water."

"Oma said you made the dean's list."

Carolyn shrugged.

Charlie straightened and studied her. "You'll make it, Carolyn. You're a survivor."

What about him? Would he make it? "I love you, Charlie. If anything happens to you . . ." She wondered if school was even important anymore.

He put his arm tight around her shoulders. She rested her head against him. He didn't make any promises this time.

When Charlie dropped her off at the door, the resident manager asked to speak with her. Two students weren't getting along. "You seem to get along with everybody. Would you mind trying another roommate?" Carolyn didn't have the nerve to say no. The RM looked relieved.

Depressed, Carolyn went upstairs, bought a Coke from the vending machine, and settled down to study. The door burst open, banging into the closet. Without apology, a girl entered and swung a duffel bag off her shoulder, flinging it onto the striped bed. "Rachel Altman." She extended her hand. "Since we're now roommates, call me Chel." She had a gravelly voice with an Eastern accent.

Startled, Carolyn shook hands. The girl had an arresting, if not beautiful, face framed by a mass of long, curling red hair held back by a woven leather headband with beaded tassels. She wore a white low-necked blouse that was nearly transparent and would have been indecent if not for the bangles and beads. A macramé belt with more beads held up skintight, brown corduroy, hip-hugging bell-bottom pants. Pulling her hand free, the girl dropped onto the bed and gave it a few experimental bounces. Her gold circle bracelets jangled. "Well, it ain't the Waldorf."

Carolyn stared, speechless. Chel looked Carolyn over, from her white Keds and socks to her ponytail. Her mouth tipped in a sardonic smile. "Let me guess. You're an education major, *primary* education. Right?"

Carolyn confessed. "What about you?"

"Liberal arts, baby. I'm liberal, and I like art. Seemed a good choice at the time, though I've been thinking about changing it to psychology or sociology. Any *-ology* would do."

"How did you guess mine?"

Chel's smile turned sly. "I just looked around. All your notes in neat little piles, typed. Books lined up. No dust on your desk. Your bed is made. All you need is a shiny apple on your desk." She flung herself backward onto the bed and put her hands behind her head. "And you're wearing a bra! I'll bet when you get dressed up, you wear a skirt and a nice sweater and pearls." She muttered a curse and lunged up, startling Carolyn again. "Don't worry, babe. I don't bite. Not girls anyway." She grinned broadly. "You look pretty uptight. You want some pot?" She laughed. "You should see your face. Haven't tried it yet, have you?" She stood and headed for the door. "Let's get out of here for a while, have coffee at the student union. I promise to be on my best behavior." She dragged Carolyn. "Come on. Live a little."

Carolyn forgot all about her studies.

Chel talked all afternoon. She seemed high on life—or something. She told Carolyn she'd grown up at the Waldorf, cared for by a well-paid but disinterested nanny while her even more disinterested daddy went off to make his millions, and her bored, disinterested mother went off to ski at Saint Moritz or buy more designer clothes in Paris. "Heaven knows where she is right now, and I couldn't care less. They're both capitalist pigs polluting the air we breathe."

She had left New York City and come to Berkeley because "Berkeley is the center of the universe, babe. It's where everything is happening! Haven't you looked around at all? I want to be in the middle of it. Don't you?"

Carolyn surprised herself and admitted she'd never had the courage to be in the middle of anything. "I've always found a way to blend in."

"A skill I obviously don't have." When Chel laughed, people looked, and she didn't care.

Carolyn had seen free spirits around the campus, but she'd never been this close to one. Chel was like an exotic bird with wild, colorful plumage who'd managed to escape from a zoo and find her way to Carolyn's dorm room. Chel fascinated Carolyn and made her laugh.

Chel looked smug. "I think you and I are going to get along real well."

She hardly saw Chel during the day, but they talked for hours when she returned from classes or wherever she'd gone. She brought pot back to the room. She put a wet towel against the bottom of the door and opened the window. "Come on, Caro. It's not going to kill you." Carolyn took a tentative puff. Chel laughed at her. *"Inhale."* After a few drags, Carolyn found herself talking. Chel lounged on her bed and kept asking questions. When asked if she'd ever had sex, Carolyn told her about Dock. Chel stopped smiling.

Despite their vast difference in material resources, Carolyn found their backgrounds weren't that different. Absentee parents who, when around, were still so preoccupied with their own problems and projects they were blind to anyone else. Of course, Mom and Dad had never been blind to Charlie. But then, Charlie was something special. She talked a lot about her brother.

"You're like a marionette, aren't you, babe? Dancing to everyone else's tune?"

No one made Chel dance.

Carolyn wanted to be just like her.

❈ ❈ ❈

1966

Once a week Carolyn received a letter from Oma, going over family news and whatever had been happening around Paxtown, which was never much. Mom called a couple of times a month, usually when Carolyn was away at class. The RM left notes in her box. *Your mom called. They're looking forward to having you home for summer break.* Carolyn groaned. She didn't want to go home, but she couldn't afford to stay in Berkeley.

"If you don't want to go home, babe, check in with the employment office. They can line up a job for you. We'll get an apartment, have some fun."

"I can't afford an apartment, Chel."

"Did I say you had to pay?"

Chel didn't let up on the idea until Carolyn gave in. She figured staying in Berkeley with Chel might be easier than explaining to her parents and Oma why her grades had dipped dramatically. Mom and Dad didn't put up a fight. That didn't surprise her. Why would they care? But when Oma didn't fuss about it, she wondered if anyone missed her. Chel told her to join the club.

Charlie, on leave after infantry training, came to visit one afternoon. He looked surprised when she answered the door. "I guess Berkeley is having its way with you."

"What's that supposed to mean?"

"Attitude, too." He grinned. "Mind if I come in? Or are you going to leave your poor brother standing out here in the hall?"

She threw herself into his arms and hugged him. "Come on in. Take a look around." Chel had rented the apartment furnished and added a few colorful pillows to the beige sofa, an Oriental rug under the coffee table. They'd nailed up posters of Venice, Paris, London, van Gogh's *Sunflowers*, and Monet's *Nympheas*, but it was Georgia O'Keeffe's *Grey Line* that dominated the living room.

Charlie gave her a troubled look. "Interesting decor."

"Glad you like it." Carolyn lounged on the couch. "Chel pays the rent. Or rather her dad does. His secretary dumps money in her account every month."

"Must be nice."

"I think she'd rather have parents who cared."

He wanted to know more about Chel. "She's the first real friend I've ever had, Charlie." She didn't want to talk behind her friend's back. "You want a glass of wine? We have Chablis or cabernet sauvignon."

"I'm driving."

She poured herself a tall glass and brought it back to the couch. He raised his brows. She lifted the glass. "Never seen a girl have a glass of wine before?" She drank deeply.

"Lots of times. Just not my little sister."

She laughed, relaxed after half a glass. She asked him a couple of questions, knowing he'd take over the conversation. He talked about training and his new buddies-in-arms. "We're all getting transferred to different bases. Dad says it was a lot different when he was in the military. They trained and went overseas as a unit. I'll be going alone."

Her muscles tightened. "Are you going to Vietnam, Charlie?"

"Not yet."

She finished the glass of wine and thought about having another. Instead, she put the glass on the coffee table and leaned her head against the sofa. She wanted to cry, but it would only make him wish he hadn't come.

Charlie tugged a strand of her hair. "Try not to worry about me so much."

She rolled her head toward him. "Do you ever worry about me, Charlie?" Did anybody?

"I will now." He leaned over and kissed her cheek before pushing to his feet. "It's getting late. I'd better get on the road. You have to work tomorrow."

Drowsy, she followed him to the door. "Tell Mom and Dad I'm doing fine." If they asked.

He grinned. "I thought I'd tell them your apartment smells like pot and you keep bottles of wine in your fridge and pornographic art on your living room wall."

"It's a flower!"

He laughed. "Yeah, right. Some flower."

She grinned, bolstered by the alcohol. "You have a dirty mind, Charlie."

"Relax. I'm not going to tell them anything. If they ask, I'll suggest they come see for themselves."

"Like they'd have time for that."

He hugged her and spoke seriously against her hair. "Don't mess around too much, okay? I'd hate for you to have regrets later on." He let her go.

She leaned in the doorway. "Didn't you mess around when you were at USC?"

"Yeah, but I'm a guy. It's permitted."

"Male chauvinist pig."

Punching the elevator button, her brother looked back at her. "Don't go too crazy, Sis." He jerked his chin up, gave her a sad smile, and disappeared into the elevator.

She went back into the apartment and poured herself another glass of wine. She cried and swore and wondered what the future held for each of them.

10

CAROLYN WENT HOME twice during the first part of her sopho-
more year, once for Thanksgiving and then for a few days during
Christmas break. Both times Mom and Dad commented on her
bell-bottom pants, embroidered blouses, leather fringed jacket, and
moccasins. She'd let her hair grow and left it hanging loose rather
than pulled back in a ponytail. They didn't approve.

"How're your classes going? Are they harder this year? What will
you be taking next?"

Carolyn had expected questions, but this felt like an interroga-
tion. "My main goal right now is to get through finals."

"What do you mean 'get through'?"

Here it comes, Carolyn thought, trying to prepare herself. "I
didn't make dean's list last time."

"We know." Mom looked as grim as she sounded.

"I don't think I'd make a good teacher. I'm thinking about
changing my major."

Dad raised his head and looked at her. "To what?"

"I was thinking about liberal arts. I'm not sure yet. I'm still trying to find myself."

Dad stared, his eyes blazing. "'Find yourself'? What's that supposed to mean?"

Carolyn wondered what her parents would say if they knew how often she went to the Fillmore or that Chel had talked her into going on the pill. Carolyn had no plans to dive into the free love movement, but Chel insisted. She could be a bulldog about some things. "Never say never, babe. And better safe than sorry." Chel wouldn't let up until she got her way, which never took long. Carolyn had always been good at giving in. Chel—charismatic, fun, smart—made it even easier.

Mom and Oma started calling more frequently and asking more questions.

They also asked when Carolyn might come home for another visit. Carolyn found excuses to stay in Berkeley.

When Mom called and said Charlie had a month's leave, Carolyn knew what it meant. He'd gotten orders to go to Southeast Asia. "He's coming home, Carolyn. I know he'd love to spend time with you."

Chel offered to drive. "Save you from taking the bus." They piled into Chel's new red Camaro purchased with "Daddy's guilt money."

As Chel turned in to the driveway, Carolyn spotted Oma working in her English flower garden. Oma stood, brushing off her hands, and shaded her eyes. Chel slowed enough that she didn't leave a cloud of dust around Oma as they passed by and parked the Camaro behind the garage next to Charlie's Impala. "Come, meet Oma." Carolyn headed for the cottage.

Oma hugged and kissed her. "It's about time you came home for a visit."

"I've been avoiding everyone." Carolyn meant it to sound like a joke. She introduced Chel.

Oma looked her over. "Would you ladies like some tea?"

"My favorite drink." Chel grinned.

As they sat at the kitchen table, Oma turned her attention to
Chel. She asked one question after another. Carolyn's stomach
tightened into a knot, waiting for her friend to say something
outrageous, but Chel didn't seem to mind the third degree. She
easily avoided questions about her parents and talked instead about
her succession of nannies and private tutors. She'd been sent off to
a boarding school in Massachusetts, then to a finishing school in
France. "I flunked out, of course, though I learned enough French
to find my way around."

"Je parle français également." Oma told her she once worked for
a French family in Montreaux and spent a few days in Paris before
going to England and then on to Montreal. Chel started asking Oma
questions; and her grandmother told of her lack of formal education, her dream of owning a restaurant and hotel, her quest to learn
languages and business skills, her journey from one job to another
to make her own way in the world. She talked about buying and
running a boardinghouse, in which her future husband boarded. "I
taught Carolyn's Opa how to speak English." She told them about
life on a prairie wheat farm and how she ended up in California.

Chel drank it all in. So did Carolyn, who had heard only bits
and pieces of Oma's story.

"Well, I've talked enough for today. You ladies had better get
over to the house before your mother thinks I'm holding you
hostage." Oma walked them to the door.

"Your grandmother is the grooviest person I've ever met!" Chel
said on the way to the house.

Charlie sat in the living room, watching television. He looked
bored when Carolyn walked in. Then he saw Chel on her heels.
Carolyn had never seen that look on his face before.

Chel dumped her backpack and stepped into the living room.
She stopped in front of him, hands on her hips as she looked
at him. "So you're the superhero Caro talks about all the time."
Speechless, Charlie stared, a bemused smile curving his lips. Chel
gave her growling laugh and cast Carolyn a catlike smile. Carolyn
didn't have to guess whether her best friend liked Charlie.

Carolyn hugged Charlie and introduced them formally. "We'd better stow our stuff in the bedroom, Chel."

Mom stood in the kitchen making dinner. Her eyes widened when she saw them. Carolyn had already warned Chel her parents were uptight, workaholic, staunch Republican, churchgoing people. Mom managed a smile and a welcome. She looked at Carolyn, a flicker of desperation in her eyes. "Your dad will be home soon. He had to go into town on an errand."

Chel tossed her pack in the corner of Carolyn's bedroom. She looked around at the pink walls, lace curtains, white chenille bedspread with pink and white pillows, and Carolyn's old rag doll. When she picked it up, Carolyn took it and put it on the dresser. "Oma made it for me."

"A woman of many talents."

They went back out to the living room. When Dad came up the drive in his squad car, Chel put her hand over her heart. "I haven't even done anything, and here come the police."

Charlie laughed. "Dad works for the sheriff's department."

She grinned at him. "I know, soldier." She glanced at Carolyn's face and leaned over to whisper. "You think he'll shoot me?"

Over the next few hours, Carolyn realized Chel could play a role perfectly. She resurrected all the manners she had been taught at the Waldorf Astoria in New York City and impressed Mom and Dad with her erudite views on the world. When Mom asked if she'd traveled much, Chel talked about a half-dozen cities in Europe, various museums, and historical sites.

Dad finally brought up politics, much to Carolyn's discomfort. Mom didn't look any happier. Chel said openly she was against the war in Vietnam and talked about how America needed changes in civil rights. When Dad opened his mouth to speak, Mom tried to change the subject. Dad scowled, aware of Mom's ploy.

Chel must have noticed too, and she trumped her. "I'd like very much to hear your opinion, sir, and how you came by it." Her sincerity seemed to surprise Dad. In the space of a second, Carolyn saw her father look past the hippy garb, the wild hair, the bangles and beads and headband, to Rachel Altman. He laid down whatever weapons he'd taken up in his mental arsenal and declared a truce by talking fondly about his days at Berkeley.

Charlie could hardly keep his eyes off Chel, though he tried to hide his fascination from Mom and Dad. Carolyn understood how easily Chel could mesmerize people. She was bewitching Mom and Dad with stories Carolyn had never heard. She wondered how many of them were true.

After dinner, Chel started to help clear the table. Mom quickly protested. Chel suggested a drive. "I'd love to see the town that shaped you, Caro." She invited Charlie, of course, but Mom and Dad came up with some lame excuse to squelch that idea. Maybe they'd noticed more than Carolyn realized.

Paxtown hadn't changed at all. They cruised Main Street like high school girls and stopped in at the Gay 90s. Chel ordered beer and flashed her fake ID so fast the waiter didn't get a good look at it, but he said he wouldn't serve Chel unless she produced a birth certificate stamped with a government seal. Unrepentant, she grinned at him. "No law against trying."

Chel wanted to see the church Carolyn's family attended. "Think it's open?" Chel got out and went up the steps to try the door. "Locked tight as a vault." The windows were too high off the ground for her to peer in. "Where else did you hang out?"

Carolyn shrugged. "That's about it."

"Looks like the eighteen hundreds around here. You wouldn't be able to sneeze in a town like this without having everyone know about it." She grinned. "No wonder you're so uptight."

"Some things go on that nobody ever knows about."

Chel looked apologetic. "I forgot about Dock." She drove down Main Street again, past the high school. "I never would've made it in a town like this."

The porch light had been left on. They took off their shoes and tiptoed into the house. Chel used the bathroom first and came out in a Cal T-shirt that hit midthigh. Carolyn went in to brush her teeth. The hall clock chimed once. She heard low voices in the hallway between her bedroom and Charlie's. When she came out, Charlie stood leaning against his doorjamb, bare-chested, pajama bottoms hanging low on his hips. She caught an odd look on his face before he straightened, wished them both a good night, and closed his door.

Later, the sound of the door opening awakened Carolyn. She saw Chel's silhouette as she went out, closing the door silently behind her. Maybe she needed to use the bathroom again. Rolling over, Carolyn went back to sleep. Chel slipped carefully back into bed just before the hall clock chimed four. "Are you okay, Chel?"

Chel jumped and let out a soft four-letter word. "I thought you were asleep."

"How many times have you gotten up tonight?"

"Once."

Once? "Where have you been?" She felt a sudden premonition and wished she hadn't asked.

"I was giving Charlie a going-away present."

The hair rose on the back of Carolyn's neck. "You didn't—"

"Relax, Caro. I asked him first." She sounded amused. "He said yes."

"If my parents ever find out . . ."

"I'll tell them I felt it my patriotic duty."

Carolyn groaned. "You're insane!"

"Maybe I am." She gave a bleak laugh. "At least, it gives me a good excuse to do what I want. You should try it sometime." She turned her back to Carolyn. "We talked, too. We didn't just—"

"I don't want to hear what you did with my brother."

"Are you mad?"

"I don't know."

"I like him, Caro. A Marine, no less." She choked up. "Who would've guessed?" She let out her breath. "I'm going back to Berkeley in the morning."

"I'm not mad, Chel. Maybe I should be, but . . . you don't have to go."

"Yes, I do. You need time with your family. They care about you."

"Yeah, right."

"Maybe you can't see it, but I can. And I'm getting out of the way."

"They were more interested in what you had to say than anything I've ever said."

"Maybe that's because you have to be drunk before you'll open up and talk to anyone." She raised herself up and peered at Carolyn. "If they didn't give a squat, they wouldn't have come home every night or taken you on every vacation. They wouldn't have moved your grandmother into a cottage next door. So don't try to tell me they didn't care." She warmed to her subject. "They call every few weeks and ask when you're coming home for a visit. You want to know the last time my dad invited me home? I can't tell you because I can't remember. The last time I saw my father face-to-face was more than two years ago."

"You get letters."

"His secretary sends a form letter once a month and encloses a check. Money, Caro, that's what I get from my parents." Her voice broke. Carolyn could hear her swallow. "Money's the cheapest, easiest gift anyone can give. If I had a hint my father or mother loved me, I'd—" She sounded angry. She spit out a four-letter word and flopped down again. "I'm going back to Berkeley, and you're staying here, if for no other reason than this might be the last time you see your brother alive."

Carolyn could feel her shaking and realized Chel was crying. She'd never seen this side of Chel before, broken, in pain. "I'm sorry. You don't have to leave."

"I can't stand seeing what I've missed, Caro, what I'll never have. What you've had all your life and don't have the sense to appreciate."

She turned over and Carolyn could tell the conversation was over. She was awake for more than an hour, wondering what would happen in the morning. What would her parents say if they found out what Chel had done? Chel would learn there was no such thing as a *Father Knows Best* or *Leave It to Beaver* family.

❄ ❄ ❄

When Carolyn awakened, Chel was gone. So was her duffel bag. Mom sat at the table with a cup of coffee. "Your friend left about an hour ago."

"Why?" Had Mom or Dad guessed what happened last night and told her to leave?

Mom shrugged. "She didn't say. She thanked us and said she had to get back to Berkeley."

Carolyn avoided her gaze. "Is Charlie up yet?"

"I guess he's sleeping in."

After the first uncomfortable moments after Charlie got up, the two of them wandered the property, talking about all sorts of things. He'd kept up with friends and filled her in on what they were doing, not that she had ever been part of their group. He talked about the Marine Corps and Vietnam and how much he believed in what he was doing. Maybe he'd stay in and make it a career, but he wasn't really thinking beyond the years of his enlistment. "How about you, Caro?" When he used Chel's nickname, she knew her friend was on his mind even if he didn't bring her up.

The whole family went to church Sunday morning. Charlie wore his uniform. He looked every inch the Marine, fit and confident. Rev. Elias announced to the congregation that Charlie was going to Vietnam. People swarmed Charlie after the service. Everyone said they would be praying for him.

Carolyn decided to skip Monday classes and stay home another day. Surprisingly, Mom and Dad didn't quibble. Dad pulled out the slide projector, and they enjoyed pictures of trips to the beach and Colorado. That night, Carolyn dreamed of Charlie in dress blues standing in a field of white crosses. Awakening abruptly, she prayed it wasn't a premonition.

Before leaving on Tuesday morning, she went over to say good-bye to Oma. They talked briefly about Chel. "That girl is headed for trouble."

"You heard her story, Oma. Despite all the money, she hasn't had an easy time of it."

"She can use her parents as an excuse to ruin her life or as a reason to do better. It's up to her."

"Is that why you shared so much of your life story with her?"

Oma tipped Carolyn's chin. "You'd better watch out for yourself, *Liebling*. If you don't decide for yourself what you want from life, someone will do it for you. And you may not like the result."

Carolyn thought that over as Charlie drove her back to Berkeley. They talked about Chel on the way. Carolyn abruptly changed the subject. "I hate the war, Charlie. I'm protesting it."

His knuckles whitened on the steering wheel. "If Dad hadn't fought, where would we be now?"

"We're not talking about World War II and the Nazis."

"We can't all stay home hoping things will turn out right."

"Vietnam isn't our country."

"We can't turn our backs on what's happening in the world, Carolyn."

"I don't care what happens to the world! I care about what happens to *my brother*. I'm going to do everything I can to get you back home."

They didn't say anything more until he pulled up in front of the apartment house. He tugged her hair. "Don't become a radical."

"Don't be a hero!" She burst into tears.

He gathered her into his arms. His voice choked as he tried to reassure her he'd come back in one piece. He set her away from him and got out of the car. He opened the trunk and took out her backpack. Leaning down, he kissed her cheek. "Try to behave yourself."

Smile dying, he looked at the door into the building. "Tell Chel I'll write."

❅ ❅ ❅

Mom and Dad continued to pay college expenses, adding fifty dollars a month so Carolyn could pay her share of the rent on the apartment. When her grades dropped, they suggested she move back into the dorm. Chel said she wasn't going back and have an RM breathing down her neck, telling her what hours she had to be in bed. But she agreed the apartment might not be such a good idea. Too many parties going on. She found a small, run-down American bungalow, furnished and within walking distance of the university, and talked Carolyn into moving in with her.

Carolyn sent her parents a change-of-address card and the new telephone number. Mom called and sounded furious. "We're not sending rent for a house, Carolyn. We can't afford it."

"You can keep your money. Chel and I have it all worked out."

"Worked out? How? She pays for everything?"

"I might quit school. Get a job. Protest the war."

"For heaven's sake, Carolyn. Don't start rebelling now. We have enough to worry about with Charlie in Vietnam."

"Which is precisely why protests are more important than classes!"

"Charlie believes in what he's doing! Your father's a veteran. How dare you speak against them! If you're going to turn into some kind of hippy, don't expect us to pay for it!" She hung up.

Carolyn held the receiver in her hand. She protested the war, not *Charlie*. And definitely not Dad. When had she ever said anything against her father's service? The hurt rose up, gripping her by the throat; and then the anger came, blistering hot, defiant. She slammed the receiver down and went into the kitchen to pour a glass of red wine. When the telephone rang again, she knew it was her mother calling back. She probably wanted to lay down more laws, make more demands, throw around more threats to make Carolyn conform.

Shaking, Carolyn downed the wine like medicine and let the phone ring.

1967

The small house became a gathering place for anyone disenchanted with the system. Carolyn went to classes when she didn't have other things to do, like canvassing the neighborhoods for signatures on petitions to stop the war, or attending protest rallies or giving blood.

As the fighting intensified in Vietnam, Carolyn grew more distracted. She flunked her midterms and stopped going to classes. She worried about Charlie all the time. She couldn't sleep. Chel encouraged her to smoke pot, but that didn't help either. Only alcohol worked, when she drank enough of it.

Mom called again. "Come home."

"You can't tell me what to do."

"Have you been drinking?"

She hadn't slept the night before, and her head felt like cotton. "What's it to you what I do?"

"Charlie would be ashamed of you!"

The words cut deeper than if her mother had wielded a butcher knife. Charlie had gotten drunk a few times after football games in high school. If Mom and Dad ever knew about it, they never said so. "I'm trying to stop the war! I'm trying to bring him home! But I guess that counts for nothing in your book! If you want to know the truth, Mom, you and Dad sent Charlie to Vietnam. All your talk of God and country."

"Stop it!"

This time, Carolyn hung up.

Dad called a few hours later. Chel answered and held out the telephone. "It's your father." Carolyn took the receiver and slammed it down.

When a letter arrived from Oma, Carolyn dreaded opening it. When she read it, she found no mention of Mom and Dad other than the usual "working hard." Oma went on about books she had read, the garden, and missing Carolyn every afternoon when she sat down to tea.

I hope you can make it home soon. I miss you.

She must be the only one. Carolyn wrote back.

Dear Oma,

I can't come home right now. I'm collecting signatures on a petition to end the war. Chel is writing for an underground press, sharing intelligence on how to protest the war more effectively. No one seems to be listening now, but I have hope that change will come. There are plans to march on Washington, and many of us are sending letters on alternative service for conscientious objectors.

Several of our friends burned their draft cards. A few are talking about moving to Canada. . . .

Carolyn thought she'd write back and argue.

Mom wrote and asked if she was coming home for Thanksgiving. Carolyn didn't answer. Mom wrote again a few weeks later and invited her home for Christmas.

Carolyn couldn't face them. She felt ashamed of her behavior, but also somewhat self-righteous as well. They didn't understand her, and with Charlie off in Vietnam, she wouldn't have an interpreter. She didn't want to face their disapproval and submit to endless lectures about her political views, her loss of faith, or whatever else they would find to criticize. She couldn't stand seeing them sitting in front of their television set, listening to the news reports and body counts. She didn't want to watch them worry and then have them take it out on her. She was doing everything she could to end the war and make a better world for all of them!

She wrote home and said she and Chel planned to go skiing in Tahoe. They had talked about it, so it technically wasn't a lie. They went to San Francisco, instead, the new happening place in America, and spent the night partying at a house in Haight-Ashbury. Cold as it was, they put flowers in their hair and danced in the streets to guitar music and bongo drums.

When they got back to the Berkeley bungalow, Carolyn had two Christmas cards, one from Mom and Dad with fifty dollars in it, and another from Oma with only a note.

Trust in the Lord with all your heart. Don't lean on your own understanding. Acknowledge Him in all your ways and He will make your path straight. Proverbs 3:5-6. Live by it and you'll have no regrets. I love you, Liebling.

Oma

Carolyn felt a sharp pang of guilt, realizing she hadn't sent a card to anyone, not even Charlie.

She wrote back.

God is dead, Oma. If He loved us, we wouldn't have wars and famines. People wouldn't die of disease or be born with deformities or mentally retarded. I don't believe in God anymore.

She sent it before she could change her mind and then felt eaten up by guilt, ashamed that she'd lashed out at Oma, who'd always loved her unconditionally.

❊ ❊ ❊

1968

January blew cold and brought with it the Chinese Lunar New Year. While the Vietnamese celebrated Tet, the Vietcong and North Vietnamese army overran the city of Hue. Chel had bought a television, and a dozen friends and strangers were packed into their living room, high on pot and angst, watching buildings explode and wounded American soldiers carried out on stretchers. Conversation buzzed around Carolyn, but she felt cold inside. Was Charlie among the Marines trying to retake the city? She wanted to scream. *Shut up! My brother is in the middle of hell, and if you call him a baby killer or warmonger again, I'll kill you.* Maybe she did say it. It got quiet in the room.

"What's with her?" someone muttered angrily.

"Jesus . . . Jesus . . . ," Carolyn prayed, trying to grasp hold of faith again, a last-ditch effort to save Charlie. *Please, God, don't let him get killed.* Drunk, she pressed her hands against the television screen. She felt someone's arms around her.

"Easy, babe. He'll be okay, Caro. You gotta believe. He'll be okay."

Believe in what? God? They'd all been saying God didn't care or God was dead. When had faith ever been enough?

Carolyn didn't go to work. She sat glued to the television, searching faces, drinking, looking for Charlie on the screen.

Oma called. "Two soldiers are with your mom and dad." She spoke Carolyn's name, but couldn't get any more out.

Something cracked inside Carolyn. She fumbled the telephone back into the cradle. Her body started to shake violently. The phone rang again. Carolyn heard it from a distance. Another sound intruded, a terrible sound, like a wounded animal screaming in pain. She covered her ears, trying to block it out. Charlie! It was Charlie!

Chel came out of the bedroom, half-dressed, hair in disarray. She grabbed Carolyn's wrists and pulled her arms down. When the sound grew louder, Chel slapped her across the face. The screaming stopped. Carolyn sat silent, stunned. Chel cupped her face. "Charlie?" Unable to speak, Carolyn crumpled. Hands spread on the bare wood floor, she sobbed.

Uttering a sobbing cry, Chel rose. She screamed a string of curses. When the telephone rang again, she grabbed the cord and yanked it out of the wall. Snatching up the telephone, she hurled it through a window. Hunkering down again, she grabbed Carolyn's shoulders and shook her. "Caro. Caro!"

The radio played an Animals song. *"We gotta get out of this place if it's the last thing we ever do. . . ."*

"I tried so hard, Chel. And I couldn't save him."

Chel got dressed, then lit a roach with shaking hands. She pulled Carolyn up with one hand and offered her the rolled marijuana. "Take a drag, Caro. Come on, babe. It's better than barbiturates."

Carolyn filled her lungs with pot smoke. She didn't want to feel anything. The music kept playing its siren song. *"We gotta get out of this place . . ."* Too late. Too late.

Chel dragged her up. "Let's get outta here."

They didn't pack anything. They left it all behind. The last thing Carolyn remembered was riding across the Bay Bridge in the front seat of Chel's red Camaro, Janis Joplin screaming, Chel screaming along with her, tears running down her white face.

Oh, Rosie, where do I begin? Charlie is dead, killed in Vietnam, and my sweet Carolyn has disappeared. The pain is too deep for tears. Hildemara can't eat or sleep; she cries all the time. I fear for her health. I fear for Carolyn as well. God alone knows where she is and what she's doing to herself. Will I lose everyone I love?

Ever since Charlie joined the Marines, the family has been in conflict. Carolyn has set herself against the war, and unwittingly against Trip. He says anyone against the war is against Charlie and every other young American boy fighting this war. Carolyn says she'd do anything to bring Charlie home, but Trip says the protests are aiding the enemy and demoralizing the troops. Trip called her a traitor and said Charlie would be ashamed of her. She withdrew from the university to devote herself to the antiwar movement, and she has no job, no means of support other than her rich, abandoned friend Rachel Altman. I've never met a more damaged girl.

Soldiers came to the house. Hildemara and Trip didn't want to call Carolyn the first day, but I called her. She hung up without saying a word, Rosie, and when I called back, she didn't answer. I assumed she was coming straight home to be with her family. She adored her brother. Charlie meant everything to her.

She never showed up. I drove to Berkeley the next day to bring her home. The house was in disarray, the telephone connection ripped from the wall, the television and several windows smashed.

I can't tell Hildemara or Trip I called Carolyn. They'd believe she didn't care enough to come home. I know the child is broken and grieving. I don't know how to find my granddaughter. I lie awake at night and I pray. When I sleep, I dream of Elise.

God knows where Carolyn is, and I pray for His mercy on all of us. I don't know what else to do.

1970

The Summer of Love had ended by the time Carolyn ran away to Haight-Ashbury with Rachel Altman after Charlie's death. Things had already begun to change. Pot still reigned, but harder drugs rose in popularity. Guru psychologist Timothy Leary advocated acid to expand the mind, but after one bad trip that left Carolyn with residual hallucinations for weeks, she made alcohol and pot her drugs of choice. She spent days in a blur, drinking liberal amounts of wine, red or white, trying to drown her grief, wash away the anger, and stop the nightmares of running through a jungle with her brother.

Chel continued to foot the bill for the two of them, in addition to a succession of hangers-on and groupies who came and went from the house they shared, many of them young men. Chel began to be haunted by hallucinations from dropping too much acid. Sobbing, she'd beg, "I need you, Caro. I need you *sober*." Carolyn tried, but craved alcohol like water. They tried to lean on one another, but it didn't help that everyone around them still used.

When the hallucinations finally stopped, they went outside and sat on the steps. Feeling the sunshine, they went to Golden Gate Park for the first time in weeks. "You've been there for me every time I've needed you, Caro, even when I didn't know what I was doing. You drove me clear across the country after Woodstock, when I couldn't have told you my name, let alone my address. We couldn't save Charlie, but you saved me. And what have I done for you?"

"You've been my friend."

"What sort of a friend am I?"

"You helped me after Charlie died."

"I should've left you in Berkeley. Your parents would have come and taken you home."

"No, they wouldn't."

"Oma, then."

Carolyn shook her head. "This is where I belong."

They found a park bench and sat. Chel put her head in her hands. "Sometimes I just want to call it quits." She gave a bleak laugh. "I'm sick and tired of being sick and tired. I'm tired of fighting a losing battle." She leaned back, hands limp in her lap. "I scare myself sometimes, Caro." She gave Carolyn a sad smile. "I don't think we've been good for each other."

Hurt, Carolyn couldn't look at her. "Am I going to lose you, too, Chel?"

"I love you, babe." Chel raised her hand in a halfhearted gesture. "See that family over there?" Her voice turned mocking. "Mommy laying out the picnic lunch while Daughter dear plays with her dolly and Daddy helps Sonny boy fly a kite? Makes a nice Hallmark card, don't you think?" Her voice choked off. She let out her breath slowly. "What do we have, Caro?"

"Our friendship."

Chel looked at her then, eyes clear for a change, wet. She looked away again. They didn't talk for a long while. "I called my father."

Surprised, Carolyn stared at her. "When?"

"A week ago. Apparently, he dumped my mother last year and

married his secretary. According to the new one, he's off on a honeymoon in Madrid."

"Where's your mother?"

"She lives in Paris. Plays in Monte Carlo. Who knows? The new secretary didn't have her telephone number, or she had orders not to give it to me. She said my father wanted to invite me to the wedding, but didn't know how to reach me." She gave a harsh laugh. "All he had to do was follow the money. He just didn't care enough."

"Maybe he figured you wouldn't want to come."

"Maybe. But it would've been nice to have the opportunity to tell him off one last time." She looked at Carolyn, eyes dark with pain. "Get this. I told that secretary I needed to talk to my father. She asked me if it was an emergency. I told her it was. She said, 'Give me your number, and I'll let Mr. Altman know you called.' I haven't heard from him yet."

"Maybe she forgot."

"She remembered. She called back. She asked me how much money I needed." She called her father a string of foul names. "He's too busy with his new trophy wife." Tears spilled down her cheeks. "If I was lying in a hospital bed, dying from an overdose, he'd tell his secretary to make sure I had a private room, private nurse, and send some flowers." She dug in her jean pocket and pulled out a worn business card. "I want you to keep this."

"Why?"

"If anything happens to me, you call my father."

Scared, Carolyn shook her head. "Nothing is going to happen to you, Chel."

"I'm not planning anything. You just never know when your time will come. I could decide to go swimming in that lake and drown. Or go down to the ocean and walk in with lead weights around my ankles."

"I don't like it when you talk so crazy."

"Don't I always?" Chel laughed again, sounding more like herself this time. "You really are something, you know that?" She cupped Carolyn's face. "I love you. You've been better to me than any sister I could've had." She dropped her hand. "Whatever happens, it's not going to be your fault." She gripped Carolyn's wrist tightly. "Remember that. It's *not your fault.*"

Worried, Carolyn kept an eye on Chel over the next few days. Chel smoked pot and drank, but not to excess. She still danced to the music, tossing her head and turning the way she had when they first came to Haight-Ashbury. Ash, the self-appointed leader of their little commune, watched Chel, too, especially when she turned up the music while he spoke his poetry. When he asked her to turn it down, she turned it up and danced right in front of him.

Carolyn thought everything would be fine then. Chel's depression had lifted. She was back to the same smirking, defiant girl she'd been in Berkeley. Carolyn went to the park for some air, spending two hours in the sunshine. She sat on a bench and watched children play, thinking of Oma and Mom and Dad. Loneliness gripped her. Pressing the heels of her hands against her eyes, she tried not to think about Charlie.

When she got back, Carolyn went upstairs and found Chel's door closed. Carolyn put her head against the door, but didn't hear voices. She tapped softly. "Chel?" She opened the door. "I've been thinking—"

Chel lay sprawled across her mattress. Her face looked so serene, Carolyn thought she was asleep. Then she noticed the rubber tubing coiled like a snake on the floor and a discarded syringe next to it. "Chel!" She knelt on the bed and lifted her. *"Chel!"* She shook her. Chel felt boneless, heavy. Sobbing her name, Carolyn let her go and screamed for help.

Voices. Footsteps running in the hall. "Everyone out!" Ash ordered. The door closed firmly. Carolyn heard the lock set. Sobbing, hysterical, she tried to speak. He clamped a hand over her mouth. When she tried to bite down, he slapped her, grabbed her by the hair, and shoved her face into the mattress. "Are you going to be quiet?" He pushed harder and only let her go when she started to pass out. Gasping for air, she scrambled away from him.

He put his hand on Chel's neck, checking for a pulse. Taking his hand away, he looked furious, not aggrieved. He swore under his breath. "Stupid witch."

"You don't even care that she's—"

"You were supposed to watch out for her." He hit her. She tasted blood in her mouth. He shoved her from him and turned toward the window.

She made it to the door, but Stoner stood right outside, blocking her escape. "What's the matter, babe?"

"Chel's dead."

"Bummer. Who's gonna pay the rent?"

She stared at him.

Ash came up behind her, his hands firm. With a tone full of compassion, he reassured Stoner. "Everything will be fine." When she tried to move away, his grip tightened. "We'll call an ambulance. Someone will come and take her to the hospital. What was her name, Stoner?"

"Chel."

When Carolyn opened her mouth, Ash's fingers bit into her flesh. "Chel." Ash spoke low. "That's all we know. Her name was Chel."

Stoner shrugged. "Yeah, man. That's all I ever knew."

Ash slipped his arm around Carolyn, pulled her back into the room, and closed Stoner out. He shoved her toward the bed where Chel lay dead. "You'll do what I tell you, Caro. Got that? It's your fault she overdosed. You said she was your friend. Where were you? You should've been right here with her every minute. I told you to keep watch." He gripped her face in viselike fingers. "But you didn't, did you? You did your own thing and had your little walk in the park. You put flowers in your hair." He crumpled them and threw them on the floor. "And now *she's* dead because *you* didn't care enough to take care of her." He let go of her and stepped away.

She'd once thought herself in love with this man. But he'd tossed her aside and moved on to another girl.

Suddenly solicitous, Ash drew Carolyn to her feet. He stroked her cheek. "It'll be the way it was." He whispered words of comfort now, words of endearment. "You don't have to worry about anything. I'll take care of you." When he kissed her, she felt nothing but revulsion. He drew back, his dark eyes searching hers. "I'll call for an ambulance. Sit with me downstairs. Be at my side." He opened the door. Stoner and several others stood waiting. "We'll light candles for our sister. We will say prayers." He stroked Carolyn's arms as though trying to smooth away the bruises.

The ambulance came within minutes. Two men got out. They unloaded a gurney and locked the vehicle doors before heading up the steps. One looked at her. When they came out with Chel's body zipped in a black bag, she heard them talking. "Chel. Not much to go by."

One unlocked and opened the back door of the ambulance. "She'll be another Jane Doe."

"Too bad. Pretty girl."

Carolyn came down the steps.

"You need to move aside, Miss."

"Her name is Rachel Altman. She came from New York City. She was an A student at UC Berkeley. They'll have her records."

His face filled with pity. "A friend of yours?"

"My best friend."

"We'll take good care of her."

"You'll be the first."

Frowning, he searched her face. "Are you going to be all right?"

Carolyn walked away without looking back. He had a job to do. So did she.

❈ ❈ ❈

It didn't take long to beg enough money for a long-distance telephone call. Carolyn stepped into a phone booth and dialed the number on the card Chel had given her. She asked for Mr. Altman.

"Who may I say is calling?"

"My name is Carolyn Arundel. His daughter, Rachel, was my best friend. She died today. You can tell him that, or let me talk to him."

"One moment, please."

Less than a minute passed and a man's voice came on the telephone. "My secretary says you have news about my daughter." He sounded annoyed. Maybe she'd interrupted a business meeting. "Make it quick. What is it this time?"

"She died of a heroin overdose this morning."

Silence. Then hushed anger. "Look. I'm in the middle of an important meeting. What kind of sick prank is she playing this time?"

"They picked up her body a few minutes ago." Carolyn gave him the Clement house address. "I gave the paramedics her full name and told them the university has her records. But Chel said if anything happened to her, she wanted me to call you. So I've called." She hung up.

Stepping out onto the sidewalk, Carolyn wasn't sure where to go. She'd been happy in the park, walking in the sunshine, looking at the flowers. She didn't make it. She walked half a block and squatted next to an old run-down Victorian row house, where she covered her head and sobbed.

She could hear Chel's voice in her head. *It's not your fault, Caro. Remember that. It's not your fault.*

Carolyn wished she could believe it.

Dear Rosie,

Trip has given up on finding Carolyn. He went to Berkeley several times looking for her, even went to the police, but they told him he is among dozens of parents whose children have "dropped out" and disappeared. Many have moved to Haight-Ashbury in San Francisco. Trip took days off work to look for Carolyn, contacting her neighbors and classmates, but so many of these young "flower children" hate authority, and Trip looks every inch the police officer he is, so I'm convinced, even if anyone knew of her whereabouts, they wouldn't tell anyone who looks like a member of "the establishment" they despise.

I am grieved Hildemara has given up on Carolyn as well. She never mentions her, nor can she abide my doing so. I invite her to tea. She declines. She comes home from work and stays in the house while Trip hammers on something. They go to church on Sunday, where they have the dubious distinction of being the only parents in Paxtown who have lost a son in action. Being a star football player in high school made Charlie a favored son, but his death has made him a local hero to some, object of hatred to others.

No one mentions Carolyn. She is more dead to everyone than Charlie could ever be.

13

Time passed in a haze of misery. With no place to go, nothing to do, Carolyn wandered through Golden Gate Park. She loitered near the museums, knowing that was her best chance of finding food. Some people looked at her with pity. Others stared in disgust, drawing children's attention away. Most pretended they didn't see her at all. She wanted a drink, but had no money. Sick to her stomach and suffering tremors, she left the pathways and collapsed. When she heard someone coming, she crawled into the bushes. Curled up in her hiding place, she wished she could will herself to die.

She used the public restrooms to wash. She found better places to sleep. Her fringed leather jacket kept the dew from soaking into her upper body, though her skirt felt wet after sleeping on the grass.

Occasionally a police car passed by. She would sit still, arms wrapped around her knees, making herself as small as possible, like an animal hiding among rhododendrons and overgrown azaleas.

She had always liked it there among the trees and flowers. The gardens reminded her of Oma's cottage.

School buses pulled in every morning during the week, bringing children for field trips. Once when the children came out to eat their bagged lunches, Carolyn approached to beg, but a chaperone told her to leave the children alone. So she sat with her back against a tree and watched children laugh, eat, and casually toss their leftovers away.

Too hungry to have any pride, Carolyn rummaged in the garbage cans, looking for their scraps. Before a security guard ordered her away, she found a half-eaten bologna sandwich, a brown banana, a box of hardened raisins. One month rolled into another. She lived hand to mouth. Her stomach was empty most of the time, but the rest of her filled up to overflowing with shame. She grieved over Chel. Worse, the anguish over Charlie's death returned. When he began haunting her dreams, she tried not to sleep at all.

❄ ❄ ❄

One evening, Carolyn went to the end of the park and down to the beach. Sitting on the cold sand, she thought about Chel. She thought about Charlie, too, all the time now. She didn't try to stop. The sun dipped toward the west. The light on the water made her eyes hurt. Her stomach ached. She hugged her knees against her chest, trying to stay warm. The surf pounded, waves whooshing up the sand while seagulls keened overhead. Two landed nearby and approached her, then flew off again when she had nothing to offer. The sky turned a beautiful rose-orange with pink streaks across the horizon.

Carolyn closed her eyes and imagined what it might feel like to walk into the surf, to go out so far there would be no turning back. She could spread her arms and drift weightless on the current until the warm water closed over her head. She imagined sinking into the blue, fish swimming around her, seaweed wrapping her in its embrace.

A blast of sand stung her face. The churning, crashing waves sounded angry, no longer inviting. The sea had come up. The mist turned cold. She got up and walked to the edge of the waves. The foamy sea lapped at her feet. In her dreams, it was warm, but this water felt ice-cold, so cold her skin and bones ached.

Courage failing, she turned away and saw a man in a military jacket sitting on the seawall, head turned toward her. Her heart quickened. Charlie? No. It couldn't be. Charlie was dead. How long had the man been there? He swung his leg over the wall and stood on the walkway. He shouldered a duffel bag and guitar case and headed back toward Golden Gate Park.

Night approached, and it grew colder on the beach. Carolyn followed the same route the man had taken. The public bathrooms had been locked. She relieved herself in the bushes and washed her hands in a public drinking fountain. Leaving the sidewalk, she crossed a lawn and sat by a small lake. Guitar music drifted on the air as one by one the stars began to appear. Carolyn moved toward the sound. She spotted a black plastic lean-to and a sleeping bag spread out beneath it. The man sat on a log, head down as he played his guitar. Hungry, cold, desperate, Carolyn swallowed her fear and approached him. He lifted his head and smiled at her. "I hoped you'd follow me."

"I like your music."

"Thanks." He had a kind smile. He was young, about the same age Charlie would be.

"Do you have any food?"

"Not much, but I'll share." He got up and dug in his duffel bag. He held out a Hershey's chocolate bar. She would have to come close to take it from his hand. "It's okay, miss. I won't hurt you." Though his face was young, his eyes looked old and sad.

"Thanks." She opened it and ate half, offering the rest to him.

"You go ahead. You can share my fire, too, if you want." He tilted his head and looked at her. "You look lost."

"Are you a vet?"

"Yeah." He went on playing the poignant, unfamiliar melody. "I'm still getting used to being a civilian."

She thought of Charlie, and tears spilled over and slipped down her cheeks. "My brother died in Vietnam."

He stopped playing and put the guitar aside. "Tell me about him."

She did. She let the words and pain flow out of her, wondering why it felt so natural to tell a stranger. She felt something happen inside her, a spark, a tiny seed of hope planted.

He told her about friends he'd lost. When he offered to share his sleeping bag, she thanked him and stretched out beside him. She didn't ask his name and didn't offer hers. The ground didn't feel as hard beneath her. When he drew the flannel-lined sleeping bag around them both, she sighed. He kissed her; she kissed him back. He was kind. He was gentle. When it was over, he didn't let her go, but held her tenderly. He cried. So did she.

She awakened once during the night, kissed him on the forehead, and walked away, the morning mist drifting through the trees. She thought she could find her way back, but she got lost again.

Exhausted, frightened, crying, she lay on the grass. She must have fallen asleep, for she awakened when someone touched her. A man whispered her name. *Oh,* she thought, relief sweeping over her, *he found me.* He stroked her hair so tenderly. Her body relaxed beneath his caress. She didn't want to move. She didn't want him to stop. Warm and drowsy, she looked across the grass. Small white flowers bloomed like stars among the green blades. He touched her again, and she felt enveloped in love.

"I've been lost."

"I know."

"I couldn't find you." She pushed herself up.

The sun rose behind him. Glorious color shone all around him. Carolyn raised a hand to shade her eyes.

"I found you." Raindrops of sensation raced up and down her body. It wasn't the young veteran who had found her. She couldn't see His face in the light, but she knew His voice even though she had never heard it before. Her heart pounded wildly. He whispered again, and then He was gone.

❄ ❄ ❄

Carolyn sat on the grass in the morning sunshine, holding tight to that one single moment when she felt loved, cherished, and for the first time in her life, certain of what she was supposed to do next.

Finally, pushing herself up, she found her way back to the sidewalk. She ducked into a public restroom to wash. Someone had broken the mirror. She stared at her reflection, like a Picasso painting, hacked up and put back together at odd angles. She dragged her fingers through her long, snarled hair, trying to make herself decent. How did she do that after spending weeks living in the same clothing, sleeping on the ground, scrounging in garbage cans? Giving up, she went back outside. She walked for a while and then sat to rest on a green lawn that tapered down to a pond.

Jesus had told her what to do. She just didn't think she had the courage to do it.

A young mother came down the slope holding a blanket and large picnic basket. A little boy and girl raced ahead of her, each with a small plastic bag in their hands. Bread crumbs for the ducks. One quickly swam their way, eight fuzzy ducklings following in her wake.

"Not so close, Charlie!"

Pain gripped Carolyn. Her heart pounded again, hard, fast, fluttering strangely as though she had just come back to life. The little boy looked older than his sister. He took her hand and pulled her away from the edge of the small lake. Protective.

Carolyn wanted to get up and move closer, but she didn't want to alarm the mother. She knew she looked a fright, like any other alcoholic still craving a drink, a slut who slept with strangers to keep warm, a derelict who ate out of garbage cans and slept under the cover of bushes. What mother in her right mind would want someone like Carolyn anywhere near her innocent children?

The young woman spread her blanket and sat down a short distance away. She smiled at Carolyn. "It's a perfect morning, isn't it?"

Carolyn found it difficult to speak. "Yes." Perfect. She watched the little boy. "You called him Charlie. My brother's name was Charlie." She turned her face away so the lady wouldn't see the tears that came so quick. She wiped them away.

"Was? Did something happen to him?"

"He was killed in Vietnam."

"When?"

"During the Tet Offensive." January 1968. Had it really been more than two years?

The lady sat for a long time, hands in her lap, watching her children. Carolyn knew she should leave, but the normalcy held her. The little boy and girl ran up the grassy slope. "Mommy! We need more bread! The ducks are still hungry!"

Chuckling, the lady opened a package of Wonder bread and handed them each a slice. "Little pieces. And don't get too close. You'll frighten them away."

Carolyn remembered Oma letting her open packages of Wonder bread on the way home from Hagstrom's grocery store. Her stomach cramped with hunger now, and her mouth watered. The children ran down the slope and threw the food to the ducks. Carolyn put her forehead on her raised knees and swallowed despair.

"Would you like a sandwich?" The lady held one out. "We have more than enough."

Too hungry to be proud, Carolyn got up and went over to accept it. "Thank you." She started to move away, but the lady spoke again.

"Why don't you sit with us and share our picnic?" She set out sandwiches, a plastic container of potato salad, a bag of chips, another container of chocolate chip cookies, pints of milk.

Carolyn sat on the grass next to the blue blanket and tried not to stare at the food as she ate the peanut butter and jelly sandwich.

"You can sit on the blanket." The lady smiled at her again. "It's all right. The grass is still a little wet with dew, isn't it?"

"I don't want to get your blanket dirty."

The lady's brown eyes softened. "Sit. Please. Do you live close by?"

Carolyn noticed the gold cross at her throat. "I've been living in the park for a while."

She looked dismayed. "Why?"

"I didn't want to go back to the place where I'd been living."

"You don't have anywhere else to go?"

Carolyn shrugged and then shook her head. "I burned my bridges a long time ago." She licked jelly off her fingers. She'd only eaten half of the sandwich. "May I please have one of those pieces of cellophane?"

"You're not going to eat the whole thing?"

"I'm saving a little. For later."

The lady's eyes grew moist. "You can eat it. I'll give you another one to save, if you want." She reached into the basket. "I wondered why I felt such an impulse to make extra sandwiches this morning." When she looked up, her eyes filled. "Don't cry or I will, too."

"People usually tell me to get lost." As if she wasn't already.

"May I ask your name?"

"Caro." A piece only, but enough.

"I'm Mary." She extended her hand. Carolyn had to move closer to shake it. "It's nice to meet you, Caro." She passed over a pint of milk, then took a paper plate and fork from the basket, scooped potato salad onto it, and handed it to Carolyn. "Tell me about yourself."

Fear melted away and loneliness won. Carolyn told Mary she had family, but they wouldn't want her anymore. She told her about college, Chel, the protest rallies, the desperation to change the world before it was too late, and then Oma's call telling her it already was. She told her about living in Haight-Ashbury and moving to Clement Street, the drinking and drugs, going to Woodstock and the long drive home wondering if Chel would make it.

"Did she?"

"Yeah. But she died of an overdose a couple months ago." Carolyn put her hands over her face and cried. "I'm sorry. I don't know why I told you all that."

"I asked, Caro. Because I care."

The children raced up the slope again. The girl came over to Carolyn. "Hello."

Carolyn felt her face fill with heat. "Hello."

"Who are you?" the boy wanted to know.

"Don't be rude, Charlie. Caro, this is Sadie, my little lady." She ran a tender hand over the little girl's dark curls. "And this is Charlie, the man of the house." Smiling, she pinched his nose. "Caro is our guest."

The little girl looked curious. "Is that why you made so many sandwiches, Mommy?"

Mary laughed. "I guess so." She patted the blanket and they sat down. They prayed together before she gave them their sandwiches.

Charlie leaned closer to his mother and whispered loudly, "Why is Caro crying?"

"Because she has had a very hard time."

"You used to cry a lot. I still hear you sometimes."

"Crying can be good for you." She kissed him. "Eat your lunch."

They took their bread crusts and ran down to the lake, eager to toss them to the ducks. Sadie, the little lady, picked tiny white flowers from the grass while Charlie went frog hunting.

"You should go home, Caro."

Carolyn hugged her knees close to her chest again and rested her forehead on them. "I don't think I'd be welcome."

"Your mother and father would want you back. So would your grandmother."

"I don't think so."

"Take my word for it. They would. They'd want to know you're alive and safe, especially . . ." She turned her face away and watched her children. "They didn't just lose their son that day, Caro. They lost you, too. I can't even imagine what I'd feel like if I lost one, let alone both my children."

"They'll never forgive me."

Mary faced her. "I'm a mother, and I can tell you no matter

what one of my children did, I'd want them to come home. I would run to them and throw my arms around them and kiss them until they cried for mercy!" She gave a soft, broken laugh. "Don't leave your mother and father wondering if you're dead or alive. That's the cruelest kind of torment."

Carolyn had a hundred excuses not to go home. She didn't have a way to get there. She'd have to beg for money for bus fare. By the time she had enough, she'd be starving again. In truth, the thought terrified her. What would Mom and Dad say? What would Oma? They'd wish her dead if they knew half of what she'd done.

Mary gathered the containers and put them back in the basket. She suddenly seemed to be in a great hurry. When she stood, Carolyn shifted off the blanket. Mary shook it out and folded it. She called Charlie and Sadie. They came reluctantly. "Do we have to go home?"

"We're not going home. We're taking Caro to the bus depot. We're going to buy her a ticket so she can go home to her family."

Carolyn gaped at her.

Mary folded the blanket over the basket and picked them up in one hand. Smiling, she held out her other hand to Carolyn and helped her up. The children ran ahead to a van parked on the road.

"Why are you helping me? Why go to all this trouble for a stranger?"

"My husband has been MIA since Tet. I don't know if he's alive or dead. I may never know." She gave Carolyn a tremulous smile, eyes awash with tears. "I can't bear the thought of someone else going through the suffering I go through every day. Don't you see, Caro? You've been MIA. You've been a prisoner of war, too. In your case, it's just a different kind of war."

"Not an honorable one. It's not the same."

"Oh, Caro. How could any mother or father not want their child back from the dead?" She grasped Carolyn's hand, squeezing it. "I'll pray they're watching for you, and they run to you when they see you coming home. If they don't, you call me. I'll come and get you."

When the depot announced her bus was about to leave, Carolyn rose. Mary and the children walked with her. Carolyn's heart pounded heavily. Her hands sweated. "You don't have to stay."

"I'm not leaving until you're safely settled on that bus and it's on its way." She scribbled her telephone number on a slip of scrap paper and handed it to Carolyn.

When Carolyn found a seat, she saw Mary, Charlie, and Sadie waving at her. She waved back.

CAROLYN GOT OFF the Greyhound bus in Paxtown and ducked into the restroom to wash her face, arms, and hands. She raked trembling fingers through her tangled hair, pulling it back over her shoulders. She didn't even own a rubber band to secure it in a ponytail. Hoping no one would recognize her, Carolyn hurried out of the bus depot and walked quickly along Main Street with her head down. She felt people stare as she passed. She wanted to run, but knew that would only attract more unwanted attention.

She breathed easier when she reached the end of town. It was a two-mile walk to Happy Valley Road, but she had been walking for weeks. Exhausted, sweaty, she headed for Oma's cottage. Mom and Dad wouldn't be home from work yet. There was a car Carolyn didn't recognize in Oma's carport, but she didn't answer when Carolyn knocked.

Carolyn didn't feel she had any right to go inside without an invitation, not anymore. She went back to the main house and lifted the flowerpot. Mom still kept the key there. She thought about going in, taking a long hot shower, washing her hair, getting something to eat. But what right did she have to go into their house? She put the flowerpot on top of the key and sat by the front door. She was so tired. If her family didn't want her, where would she go? She awakened sharply when a car came up the gravel driveway. The hedge had grown high, and she couldn't see whether it was Mom or Dad. Footsteps crunched in the pebbles, soft footsteps. Mom. Carolyn stood slowly, heart pounding.

Her mother came around the corner, looking so familiar and professional in her white uniform and cap. Startled, Mom stopped. She stared at Carolyn and took a step back. Then her eyes went wide. "Carolyn?" Before Carolyn could speak, Mom dropped her purse and flew at her. Carolyn cringed, expecting a blow, but found herself in a fierce embrace. Uttering a sobbing gasp, her mother let go and stepped back. "I didn't know it was you at first. You're so . . . different."

Different wasn't the word.

"When did you get home? How did you get here? Where have you been? What happened? We've been—" She stopped abruptly, her eyes sweeping over Carolyn. She raised her hands. "Never mind." She frowned in confusion. "Why didn't you go inside? The key . . ."

Carolyn didn't know what to say.

"It's okay." Mom spoke quickly. She unlocked the door and pushed it open. "Come inside." She remembered her purse and went back for it. Holding her elbows, Carolyn waited just inside the door. "Come in." Mom threw her purse on the breakfast counter and started to pull out the bobby pins that held her nurse's cap in place. She headed for the back of the house. Mom always took a shower immediately after coming home from the hospital.

Mom stopped and wheeled around. She looked scared. "Don't leave, Carolyn."

"I won't."

"Promise me!"

"I promise."

Mom let out her breath. "Okay. I'll only be a few minutes."

A few minutes might be all her mother needed to change her mind about letting Carolyn into the house. And what then? Carolyn stood in the entry hall and raised her head. She caught her breath at the memorial wall in front of her.

An eleven-by-fourteen picture of Charlie in his dress blues smiled at her. Two small potted palms sat on either side of the elaborate gilt-framed portrait sitting on a shiny black table. The wall above was covered with framed photographs: Charlie as a baby, Charlie as a toddler on his tricycle, Charlie and Mitch standing by their bikes, Charlie and Mitch in their high school football uniforms, Charlie showing off his varsity sweater, Charlie in black cap and gown holding his high school diploma and scholastic award, Charlie in his Trojan football uniform, Charlie looking handsome in Marine greens. The pictures surrounded a glass-encased triangular folded American flag set against black velvet. Below it were several colorful military ribbons, a Bronze Star, and a snapshot of Charlie grinning broadly, arms flung around two Marine buddies, a bunker and palm trees in the background.

Carolyn's throat closed tight and hot. If she lived a hundred years, she'd never get over losing Charlie.

The foyer felt warm, sunlight shining in from the skylight. She glanced into the living room. Everything looked exactly the same as the day she had left home: curved beige couch and oval birch coffee table in front of the wall fireplace, two recliners with a table, the television set.

"Carolyn?"

She turned slowly, steeling herself for whatever her mother might do next. She'd changed into blue polyester pants and a red, white, and blue polyester blouse. Her mother had every right to scream at her and tell her to go back to whatever hole she'd been hiding in for the past thirty months. They stood staring at one another, both at a loss for words.

Carolyn chewed her lower lip and gathered enough courage to speak. "Can I use the bathroom, Mom? Would you mind if I took a shower?"

Mom blinked. "Yes. Of course." She pointed as though Carolyn might not remember the way.

Stripping off her tan leather jacket, tiered peasant skirt, and blouse, she stepped into the stream of hot water. It felt so good. She squirted Prell shampoo into her hand and scrubbed her hair. She lathered and scrubbed her body, washing until the water at her feet ran clear. Then she just stood and let the water beat down on her until it went from hot to lukewarm.

After drying off, she wrapped the towel around herself and found a toothbrush and Colgate toothpaste in the drawer. How long since she'd brushed her teeth? Her gums bled.

Gathering her clothes, she went into her bedroom. Nothing had changed in here either. She slid the closet door open and saw two dresses, a jumper, a few skirts and blouses she'd worn in high school, things she hadn't wanted to take to Berkeley. She found underwear, faded jeans, and Charlie's discarded purple and gold high school sweatshirt. He'd tossed it at her the day he graduated. *"It's all yours, Sis."* She could hear the echo of his voice.

The jeans hung loose on her hips. She found a pink belt in the closet and cinched it to the last hole, bunching the denim around her waist. The sweatshirt looked huge on her. She put her arms around herself, thinking of Charlie.

A brush and comb were still in the top drawer. Her scalp stung as she brushed the tangles from her hair. If she'd found scissors, she would have cut it all off, hacked it away in penance. It hung damp and limp to her waist, a curling mass of sun-bleached blonde. She couldn't stop shivering. Ice ran in her veins.

Charlie. Chel. Both dead.

She went out to face Mom. Carolyn could hear the *click, click, click* of the potato peeler and followed the sound to the kitchen. Strips of potato peelings flew into the sink. Six naked white orbs sat on the counter. Did they have company coming to dinner? Mom glanced over her shoulder. "There you are. How was your shower?"

"Nice."

"I put a roast on. Dad will be home in an hour. It'll be a while before we can eat. Do you want anything now?"

"A glass of milk?"

"Help yourself."

Carolyn poured a full glass and drank it without stopping. She felt Mom watching her.

"You look exhausted." Mom bit her lip. She peeled another potato and then made a sound of disgust. Tossing the peeler aside, she scooped up the potato peels and dumped them in her compost bucket under the sink. "I don't know what I'm thinking. Well, we'll have leftover potatoes for a few days, I guess." She gripped the edge of the sink and stared out the kitchen window. "Where have you been all this time?"

"San Francisco." Light-headed, Carolyn swayed.

Mom had hold of her before she knew her mother had even moved. "Why don't you lie down and take a nap? I'll wake you when it's time."

Time for what? To face her father? Time for Mom to get over the initial shock of having her daughter show up on the front doorstep like a filthy stray cat?

"Come on." Mom kept her arm firmly around Carolyn's waist. When they went into Carolyn's old bedroom, Mom let go of her and yanked back the covers. "Lie down before you fall down!" She pulled the covers up over Carolyn's shoulders. Carolyn felt her mother's cool hand on her forehead. "Sleep for a while."

She heard the sound of voices, but couldn't quite rouse herself. Someone kissed her forehead. She thought she smelled her father's Old Spice. More whispered voices. Then she sank into a dark pit and stayed there.

❄ ❄ ❄

Carolyn saw sunlight streaming in the bedroom window. How long had she slept? Her heart stopped when she heard Dad's voice.

She wanted to cover her head with the blankets and go back to sleep. But she couldn't hide forever.

She opened her door carefully and slipped into the bathroom while her parents talked in the kitchen. When she came out, she opened the door to Charlie's bedroom and stepped inside.

His bed still had the same blue spread. The red blaze roses bloomed around his window. His Monopoly game had been laid out on his desk, money neatly stacked on both sides of the board, as though he and a friend had just left the game. There were hotels on Boardwalk and Park Place.

A USC banner hung on the wall. The bookshelf Dad had built still held Charlie's favorite sci-fi novels. She opened his closet. His shirts and slacks still hung there. She stepped inside and held a shirt to her face, breathing in the fading scent of her brother. She took it off the hanger and sat on his bed, holding the shirt to her face. If she closed her eyes, she could pretend he still lived in this room, had just gone out for a drive in his red Impala.

Gulping down a sob, she bunched the shirt against her mouth to stifle the sound. If she'd been anywhere else, out of sight, alone, she might have keened and wailed and screamed the way she had the day she learned her brother had been killed. She might have torn her clothes and ripped at her hair, might have slashed herself with a knife, anything to release the balled-up, tight-fisted, raging grief inside her.

Jesus. Jesus! Why Charlie? Why not me? He had so much going for him. And I'm nothing.

She thought of all the things she'd done in the last three years and wondered if a person could die of shame.

"Carolyn?" Mom stood in the doorway, her face pale and strained.

"I'm sorry." Carolyn stood, legs shaky. She held Charlie's shirt clenched in one hand. If Mom tried to take it from her, she'd hang on and fight for it.

"Breakfast is ready."

Breakfast? Hadn't she been peeling potatoes for dinner?

Dad sat at the kitchen table. Charlie's death had aged him. His hair had turned gray at the temples, and he had new lines across his forehead, around his eyes, and in his cheeks, lines carved by sorrow. She met his eyes briefly and bowed her head. He started to rise and seemed to change his mind. He put his hand flat on the table. "Sit down."

Mom set two plates on the table, one in front of Dad, one in front of Carolyn. Carolyn stared at the mound of scrambled eggs, four strips of bacon, a blueberry muffin. Mom filled her glass with orange juice. She couldn't remember the last time she'd had juice.

Setting her own plate on the table, Mom sat. Dad said grace.

"You slept thirty-six hours."

Carolyn raised her head and looked at her father.

"You must've needed it." He forked eggs into his mouth, not looking at her.

"You need to eat, too." Mom waved at the plate.

Carolyn's hand shook when she picked up the fork, and her teeth hurt when she chewed. Her throat felt so dry she had to swallow orange juice to wash down the muffin. Though they didn't stare, she felt her parents' attention fixed on her. What thoughts ran through their heads? What names did they want to call her? *Druggie. Boozer. Hippy. Worthless slut.*

All true.

They didn't ask questions; the silence became excruciating. She'd prepared herself for anger, accusations, fury, fingers pointed at the door, but not this watchful tension, this nervous caution.

She'd been sent home by Jesus, bus fare paid by one of His saints. Now what? What could she say? What excuses could she offer?

She couldn't eat any more. She put her fork down carefully, head still bowed. She put her hands on the table, meaning to push the chair back. Dad grabbed her hand, pinning her at the table. "We're glad you came home, Carolyn." His voice sounded rough and hoarse. "You know that, don't you?"

She raised her head and looked at him.

"We're glad you're home," he repeated.

She pulled her hand away and covered her face. She gulped down a sob.

How long had she been running on empty? Since she'd run from Berkeley . . . or long before that? She'd tried to fill the void, but nothing had worked—not alcohol, not drugs, not sex. All of it emptied her even more.

She had one miraculous moment to cling to in all that mess. One single minute at dawn, the May flowers blooming like stars in the grass, and Jesus laying His hand on her head. Telling her it was time to go home.

Jesus. They'd never believe it, not in a thousand years. They'd think she'd had some kind of drug-induced hallucination.

A sound came out of Dad, ripped out.

"Trip." Mom spoke, frightened.

He pulled Carolyn's chair back. When she almost fell, he swept her up and sat down again with her in his lap. Hugging her tight against him, he wept.

15

Mom and Dad stayed home from work. She knew they wanted to ask why she had disappeared, but didn't, perhaps waiting for her to volunteer the information. She hadn't been thinking about them, the grief they must have suffered, and the further grief she might cause. She hadn't thought about anything at all. How could she tell them that she simply couldn't bear seeing Charlie in a coffin?

"Oma's visiting Rikka back in New York. Your aunt is having another showing. We called them last night to let them know you'd come home."

What would Oma say when she returned?

"I went to San Francisco a half-dozen times," Dad told her. "I thought you might be in Haight-Ashbury."

She'd been drunk or stoned most of the time. She hadn't even stepped outside the house that first month. They left shortly after that. "Chel and I lived on Clement Street."

"Is she still there?" Dad sounded worried. Maybe he thought she'd change her mind and go back.

"She died of an overdose."

"What a waste." Mom's words summed up everything.

They gave up trying to make conversation and did chores around the house. Carolyn felt at loose ends, not knowing what to do. When she tried to help with the dishes, Mom told her to go into the living room and relax, but Dad had the TV on and Carolyn didn't want to hear the news. The Vietnam War was still going strong, more unpopular than ever.

She took a nap in the afternoon. Even after hours of sleep, she felt tired.

Mom awakened her. "Dad just brought Oma home from the airport. Why don't you go over and say hello?"

Oma stood on her front porch, watching Carolyn walk across the lawn. Dad gave her an encouraging smile as he headed for the house. When Carolyn came close, Oma put her hands on her hips. *"Die Verlorene kommt schliesslich nach Hause."*

Carolyn gave her a bleak look.

"I said, 'The prodigal finally comes home.'" She let out her breath. "I'd like to beat you to within an inch of your life, but you already look like you've been through enough. Come inside. We'll have some tea and talk."

Oma filled the teakettle and slammed it on the stove. She spoke German again and corrected herself. "I haven't any cookies, not even store-bought. Tomorrow, I'll make a cake. You look terrible. Did they tell you that?"

"No."

"Well, you do. You're skin and bones! What have you been eating? air?"

"Trash."

Oma scowled. "You look it. Do you know what you've done to your mother and father and me with all your foolishness?"

"I'm sorry."

"Sorry. *Sorry!*" She closed her eyes and shook her head. She sank into the chair as though her legs wouldn't hold her up anymore. "It was my fault. I should have come to Berkeley and told you in person, brought you home with me."

"It wasn't your fault, Oma."

"Tell me where you've been all this time and what you've been doing." She waved her hand. "And I don't mean San Francisco."

"You don't want to know, Oma. You really don't." Carolyn struggled to keep tears back.

She sighed heavily. "I guess it's none of my business anyway." She raised her head. "What happened to Chel?"

Leave it to Oma to ask. "Heroin overdose." Carolyn swallowed hard. "Suicide."

Oma looked ready to cry. "Too many young people are dying these days."

"Where's Charlie buried?" Carolyn hadn't dared ask her parents.

"He could've been buried at Arlington, but your parents wanted him up on the hill, close to home." Carolyn thought about Charlie and figured Mom and Dad had made the right decision. "Hildemara—" Oma corrected herself. "Your mother went up every day for the first year."

"Can I take some flowers when I go?"

"Cut as many as you want. Anytime." Oma got up and poured hot water over the tea bags and set the cups on the table. "Take a bottle of water along. You'll need to refill the vase."

They sipped tea together. Oma set her cup down. "What do you plan to do now?"

"I don't have any idea."

"You're going to have to do something. Sitting around is the worst thing you can do for yourself."

"I know."

Oma stood behind her, stroking her shoulders. She held Carolyn's head and kissed her crown like a blessing. "Every day is a new beginning, *Liebling*."

❄ ❄ ❄

Carolyn heard Mom and Dad talking in the morning.

"Maybe I should stay home a few more days."

"You can't keep watch forever, Hildie. Besides, your mother will be here. She'll keep an eye on her."

When Carolyn opened the door, they stopped talking. Dad was wearing his uniform. She felt relieved to see him in it. They'd been treating her like a guest.

"I've got to go into town and do some grocery shopping." Mom sounded apologetic. "Would you like to go with me?"

And have everyone in town staring at her? "I'd rather stay here."

After they both left, Carolyn went through the house. She couldn't find a single picture of herself anywhere. Mom and Dad might have had only one child—Charlie.

She wrote a note and left it on the kitchen counter. She went over and cut flowers from Oma's garden and walked to the cemetery. The gate had been opened so people could drive in, make the loop, and come out. Few did. Carolyn had been here before, exploring with Charlie, and never seen the caretaker.

It took some wandering before she found Charlie's grave. He rested on the slope facing town, a row up from the iron fence, a small American flag on the headstone.

Kneeling, Carolyn removed the dead flowers, refilled the black vase with water, and arranged the fresh bouquet. Looking at the patches of golden California poppies and blue and white lupines dripping like splashed paint down the hillside, she started to talk. She cried, too. She told her brother how she'd run away the day she heard he'd been killed. She told him about the veteran she met in the park and Jesus touching her in the morning. She told him about Mary and little Charlie and Sadie and the ducks swimming on the pond.

After a while, she even told him about Dock.

She felt better for all of it, purged.

Oma stood at the end of the drive, taking mail out of the box. "You must be hungry. You've been gone for hours. Come on up to the cottage. I'll fix you lunch." She sorted the mail as they walked up the driveway together. "Your mom called. She was worried when you didn't answer the phone."

"I left a note."

"I know. I saw it. I called and let her know where you went."

"I confessed all my sins to Charlie." She tried to make light of it.

"He'll keep your secrets." She handed her a few envelopes. "Put those on the kitchen counter and come on over."

After lunch, Carolyn sat on the floor in Oma's small living room and fingered puzzle pieces. She raked fingers through her hair and stared at the hundreds of pieces. Nothing seemed to fit. "I don't know what I'm going to do, Oma."

"You're going to eat right and get your health back. You're going to stop kicking yourself. You're going to get up and put one foot in front of the other and get on with your life. That's what we all have to do."

"You make it sound easy."

"Nothing is easy, Carolyn. Life isn't easy. We do the best we can with what God gives us."

"I've made a complete mess of everything."

"It's not about what you've done. It's about what you're going to do now."

※ ※ ※

Mom, Dad, and Oma took her to church. Everyone greeted her parents affectionately and then greeted her, too, eyes curious. Some talked about how they remembered her as a little girl.

"So shy and quiet. Such a pretty little thing."

"I remember when you came to my Sunday school class the first time. You didn't say a single word. You haven't changed much."

A lie they all wanted to live with.

Oma tucked her arm through Carolyn's and stood closer. "Why don't we find a seat?"

Carolyn felt strangely at home. She closed her eyes and listened to the choir. She listened so intently to Rev. Elias's prayer, she felt as though she knew what words he'd speak before he said them. She listened to every word of the sermon. The message seemed to have new meaning after her experience in the park. She knew the One he talked about now. It all made sense. She had been blind. Now, she could see, even with her eyes closed. She had been deaf; now she could hear.

When the service ended, Carolyn made the long walk to the back door, where Rev. Elias stood, accepting parishioners' thanks for an excellent sermon. He spoke warmly to her parents and Oma. The smile didn't reach his eyes when he looked at her. "Carolyn."

"It was a wonderful sermon, Rev. Elias."

"How would you know? You slept through it." He spoke tersely, then smiled at the people behind her. She took the hint and went out the door and down the steps.

Carolyn kept going to church, but kept her eyes open. She looked at Rev. Elias, hoping he knew she was paying close attention. She didn't feel Jesus' presence in the building, although she saw Him in her parents and Oma and some of the people who talked with her. She felt closer to God in the cemetery sitting beside Charlie's grave or sitting on the swing her father had built. And she clung to the memory of her encounter with God in Golden Gate Park at dawn, May flowers blooming in the grass.

God loved her, even if no one else could.

16

Mom and Dad's friend and dentist, Doc Martin, offered Carolyn a job as his receptionist, the last girl having quit the week Carolyn came home from San Francisco. Thelma, Doc's wife, worked as the hygienist. Carolyn learned quickly that Thelma knew everyone's business and didn't mind sharing.

About a month into her job, Carolyn started to get nauseated every time she came to work. She'd always been bothered by the sounds of drills; now the scents turned her stomach. She tried to keep busy answering phone calls, calling patients to remind them of appointments, taking messages, but the smell of hot enamel sent her running for the bathroom.

Thelma tapped on the door. "Are you all right, Carolyn?"

She retched again. "I'll be out in a minute, Mrs. Martin." Fighting the nausea, she waited a moment and hoped her stomach wouldn't heave again. She'd already lost her eggs and toast. Nothing else remained. She rinsed her mouth, patted her face with a damp paper towel, and opened the door.

Thelma stood right outside, expression curious. "You look awfully pale."

"I'll be all right." The telephone rang and she hurried to answer. Feeling woozy, she slid quickly into the office chair and picked up her pencil. She could feel Thelma's eyes fixed on her back. She jotted another message on the pad.

By lunchtime, she felt fine. The next morning, she felt sick again, and the morning after that. She wondered if she had grown allergic to something in Doc Martin's office. Thelma, maybe. Just being around the woman made Carolyn anxious, but the thought of having to look for another job made her even more so.

When she threw up Saturday morning, she knew it didn't have anything to do with the scents and sounds of the dentist's office. So what was it? Mom heard her heaving and suggested saltines and 7UP. "They'll settle your stomach." They did.

At church the next morning, she had to leave the service. She barely made it outside before she puked in the bushes next to the front steps. Mortified, gulping for air, she straightened and saw her mother standing on the steps above her. "I think I need to lie down in the car, Mom."

Mom walked her to the car. "How long has this been going on, Carolyn?"

"Two weeks."

She paled noticeably. "*Every* morning?"

Carolyn shrugged. "It's probably a flu bug or something."

"I don't think so." Mom looked stricken. "As if things aren't bad enough already." She opened the car door. "We're going to have to talk about this later. Don't say a word about it to anyone, not even Oma, and especially not your father. Not yet."

Carolyn slipped into the car.

"Let's just hope you're not pregnant." Mom slammed the door and headed back to church.

Carolyn fought another wave of nausea. Pregnant? Ash had used her for weeks, but that had been months ago. After him, she hadn't wanted anyone to touch her ever again. She'd been on the pill up until she left the Clement Street house. She'd left everything behind that day, but why would she have needed birth control when she stayed clear of people, except to beg?

The young veteran sitting on the seawall the night she wanted to commit suicide. He played the guitar. He'd given her a candy bar. They'd talked. He kept her warm all night.

She understood now why Mom had that look on her face, why she looked ready to curse and cry, why she thought things were going to get worse.

Curling up on the backseat, Carolyn wept.

❄ ❄ ❄

Dr. Griffith confirmed Mom's suspicions. "She's about six weeks along. I think it'd be wise to check for VD."

Dad sat stunned at the dining room table. He looked like someone had punched him in the stomach. Pain first, then anger. He punched back. Hard. "Do you even know who fathered it?" He didn't wait for an answer before cursing her. Mom whispered his name in an agonized voice, but he didn't hold back. "Charlie would be ashamed to call you his sister! It's better he's dead so he can't see what you've become." He put his head in his hands and wept.

Charlie had died honorably, a hero deserving of a shrine. No shrine for Carolyn. She hadn't seen a picture anywhere in the house, and she had looked. It would be worse now that she was the cause of the second-worst catastrophe a parent could suffer. "I'm sorry. I should've stayed in San Francisco." She'd probably be dead by now, but maybe that would've been easier on everyone.

"Why didn't you say something?"

She looked at Mom. "I didn't know." Not that that was any excuse. She felt the muscles tightening around her throat as though her own body tried to strangle her. The pain kept getting worse. She pushed it down the way she'd always done, but it was harder this time.

Dad scraped his chair back. "Maybe you're right. Maybe you should've stayed in San Francisco. Maybe you should go back!"

"Trip!" Mom's voice cracked.

"How are we supposed to fix the mess she's made of her life? Tell me that!"

"Trip . . ."

He glared at Carolyn. "Get out of my sight!"

Carolyn got up and headed for the front door. Mom cried out, *"No!"* She came after Carolyn and gripped her by the elbow. "Don't leave. Just sit in your room for a while; let me talk to him." Carolyn turned like an automaton, guided by her mother's firm hand.

Closed in, curled up on her bed, pillow over her head, she could still hear them shouting.

Chel came to her in her dreams that night. She walked into the surf. When she reached waist level, she turned and held out her hand. Carolyn followed. As the sea closed over her, she found she could still breathe. She swam among the seaweed, feeling the silky strands try to catch hold. She saw the young vet at the bottom playing the guitar. Charlie sat and listened. Chel sea-danced, her red hair floating around her.

When she got up in the morning, Dad sat at the dining room table. She hesitated and stepped back. Dad glanced at her. "Sit down, Carolyn." Steeling herself for further judgment and condemnation, Carolyn obeyed. She was only getting what she deserved.

Dad looked miserable. "We'll figure things out."

Mom sat down with them. "We'll just carry on as usual. You'll keep going to work. Dr. Griffith won't say anything to anyone."

"Mom is going to make a few calls, see what she can find out about homes for unwed mothers."

It didn't surprise Carolyn that they would want to get rid of her, but it still hurt. She had deserted them at the worst time in their lives, and now she came back and presented them with more trouble than they ever deserved. What right did she have to expect them to help her through this crisis?

"It'll be some time before you show." Dad could barely get the words out. "At least we can keep it secret for a while."

Mom folded her hands on the table, knuckles white. "We don't have to make all the decisions now." She searched Carolyn's face, her own troubled. "Is there anything you want to say, Carolyn?"

Instinctively, Carolyn covered her womb. Only one thing mattered to her now. "My life is completely . . ." She used a foul expression she had never heard come from either of their lips, but had heard every hour of every day in her other life. "Please don't take it out on my baby." She got up and fled to her room.

❄ ❄ ❄

No one had to tell Thelma Martin the news. "You're pregnant, aren't you?"

It wasn't really a question. She could sniff out gossip faster than a bloodhound could catch the scent of an escaped prisoner. One of her chatty friends had been sitting in Dr. Griffith's waiting room and saw Mom's face before they left.

"I can see the guilt on your face. Your poor parents . . ." False sympathy oozed from her voice. "I'm so sorry about what they must be going through, Carolyn, but we can't have you working here. Not in your—" her lips pursed—"*condition*. People would think we approved." Thelma's eyes glinted.

When the telephone rang, Carolyn didn't answer it, but rather picked up her purse, took her sweater off the back of the chair, and headed for the door.

"Where do you think you're going?" Thelma demanded, loud enough for the two waiting patients to hear.

"Home."

"Answer the telephone."

"You just fired me. You answer it."

"I didn't mean you had to leave *today!*"

As Carolyn headed for Charlie's red Impala, she imagined what

Chel might say. Her friend would've known how to rock and shock Thelma enough to leave her speechless.

She drove home, hoping to get into the house and close herself in her room, where she could think, before Mom and Dad heard. Maybe she'd be safe for a few hours before the crap hit the fan. By tomorrow morning, the stench of her life would be all over town.

Oma called out to her. Carolyn wanted to pretend she didn't hear. "Carolyn!"

She stopped and closed her eyes for a second, wondering if Oma had heard the news yet. Why not tell her? She might as well get it over with and have the last member of her immediate family hate her.

"I'm pregnant. And no, I don't know who the father is. Mom and Dad wanted to keep it secret. Thelma figured it out. So the cat's out of bag. I just got fired. So much for Mom and Dad saving face by dumping me in an unwed mothers' home before the whole town knows."

Oma said something in German.

Dropping to her knees in the gravel driveway, Carolyn sobbed. She felt the sharp pain of stones cutting into her flesh.

Oma's strong hands pulled her tight against her. "It's not the end of the world."

❄ ❄ ❄

Mom and Dad sat in silence as they heard the news. Oma told them. Having spent most of the afternoon hugging the porcelain throne, Carolyn barely managed to sit at the table. She didn't eat, and neither did Mom and Dad after they heard Thelma Martin knew everything. Or thought she did. Carolyn kept her head down. "I'll find another job."

"What's the point?" Dad threw his napkin on the table. "Who'd hire you now?"

"That's a nice thing to say." Oma sounded disgusted and angry.

Mom sighed heavily. "Thelma Martin is the biggest gossip in town. It's bad luck Carolyn ended up working for them."

Dad looked at Mom. "Have you been able to find out anything about homes?"

"I have another idea, but I need a little more time."

Carolyn suspected she knew. She didn't want to add an even bigger sin to all the rest she had committed. "I won't have an abortion."

Mom and Dad stared at her. "We wouldn't suggest such a thing." Mom spoke for both of them, but the guilt on their faces told Carolyn they'd already debated that solution. "Just stay home until we can sort this out."

Oma left the table, slamming the front door as she went out.

❄ ❄ ❄

Over the next week, Carolyn watched her parents try to live a normal life. They went to work; Carolyn stayed home. Oma invited Carolyn to ride into town with her while she ran errands, but Carolyn declined. If Mom and Dad didn't want her showing her face, she wouldn't.

When Sunday rolled around, they shocked her by saying they wanted her to come to church with them. "Why?" She couldn't think of a worse idea. Thelma Martin was one of the deaconesses.

Mom looked determined. "People know what Thelma Martin is. And there are more people in that church than one nasty gossip." Clearly, she had a point to make, and it didn't matter how Carolyn felt. "You're not staying home."

People greeted them. Some gave pitying glances; others seemed embarrassed; most said nothing, just gave a nod and a faint smile. Mom led the way to the same pew they had occupied for years, six rows from the front, where they could see and hear everything. Oma told Carolyn to keep her head up. Rev. Elias stepped to the pulpit and gazed down at Carolyn, and then he looked at the rest of his congregants.

When the service ended, Carolyn just wanted to escape. Mom and Dad worked their way toward the door, where Rev. Elias stood. Carolyn saw Thelma whispering to several women. Oma stopped and glared at them.

Carolyn noticed her parents saying a quick, quiet word to Rev. Elias as they reached the door. He nodded grimly, shook Dad's hand, and patted Mom sympathetically. Oma took Carolyn's hand and pulled it through her arm. As they came to the door, Rev. Elias smiled at Oma, but ignored Carolyn. When he extended his hand to Oma, she ignored it and walked out the door.

"I'd like to shoot Thelma Martin." Mom stared out the window.

Dad started the ignition. "She's not saying anything that isn't true."

Mom and Dad went back to town that afternoon. Mom came home red-eyed from crying, but she was more serene than she had been in days. Dad seemed more relaxed, too. "Rev. Elias wants to talk with you, Carolyn. Monday is his day off. He said one o'clock would be convenient."

The church door stood ajar when Carolyn arrived. She stepped into the narthex and saw Rev. Elias in his office, writing on a legal pad. Tapping lightly, she waited for permission to enter. After several minutes, he tossed his pen on the desk, sighed heavily, and looked at her. "Come in." He sounded grim. "Sit down." Leaning forward, he steepled his fingers. "Your parents and I talked yesterday. Did they tell you?"

"No, sir." But she'd known, all the same.

"We had a long talk. I've never seen your father cry. You've broken their hearts. Mine, too." He sat back in his big chair. "I wonder if you have any idea how we feel. I've watched you grow up. I had such hopes. They brought you to Sunday school; they brought you to youth group; they've done everything possible to rear their daughter as a moral, upright, responsible girl. You've disappointed all of us, Carolyn, everyone in the congregation."

"I've disappointed myself, sir."

"Oh, let's not play games, shall we?" His tone hardened. "I

know what goes on in Haight-Ashbury. I can imagine what you've been doing since you took off. 'Doing your own thing.' Isn't that what you call it? And then you came back. I hoped. We all did. I thought maybe you'd repent. But then I saw you sitting in the pew with your eyes closed. You don't like hearing the truth, do you? You don't want to listen to the Word of God."

"I pray—"

"Don't lie to me. I wasn't born yesterday." He shook his head, mouth tight. "I confronted you. And you stared at me after that. Open defiance. I can see everything from where I stand. I can see *you.*"

Her body grew colder as his tone grew hotter.

"You can look like a Christian on the outside, but it's the fruit that shows what you are." His gaze flickered down, resting pointedly on her abdomen, then back up to stare coldly into her eyes. "You can't hide now, can you? Everyone will know what you are."

She didn't think it could get worse, but he wasn't finished.

"When your brother died, you didn't even have the decency to come home for his funeral. You didn't care enough to show him the honor he deserved. You wanted your own way. Now you have to live with the consequences."

She bowed her head and cried.

"You're sorry now." Rev. Elias sounded weary. "You have regrets; you feel remorse. But I have yet to hear your confession. I see no evidence of repentance."

What kind of evidence did he want? She was about to ask, but one look at his face kept her silent. She didn't see even a hint of love or compassion in his eyes. He'd been the only pastor she'd ever known, but as she searched for Jesus in his face, she couldn't find Him.

The wall clock *tick, tick, tick*ed.

"Well, Carolyn? Don't you have anything to say? Or do you think it's all water under the bridge?"

What could she say? She had sinned, she was paying, and she'd keep paying as long as she lived.

Rev. Elias let out an impatient sigh. "Go on then. Have it your way. I'll pray for your mother and your father, but I won't pray for you. I'm giving you over to Satan. Let the devil sift you."

Carolyn sat in Charlie's Impala, gripping the steering wheel. She wanted a drink. Not just one, a whole bottle, and it didn't matter if it was wine or whiskey. She wanted a drink so badly, she shook and broke out in a cold sweat. She wanted a joint. She wanted acid. She wanted oblivion!

The only thing that stopped her from driving to Hagstrom's grocery store and buying booze was the child tucked beneath her heart.

When Carolyn entered the house, Mom stood in the kitchen fixing dinner; Dad stood nearby talking with her. Mom glanced over her shoulder. "Did you have your talk with Rev. Elias?" She sounded hopeful.

"Yes."

Dad's mouth tightened. "I hope you took everything he said to heart."

"I have." She'd never set foot in a church again.

Carolyn went into her bedroom and closed the door. She thought she might have some respite, but Dad tapped on her door and said to come out in the living room. They had something to tell her. She went on leaden legs.

Dad sat, hands gripping the arms of his recliner. Mom spoke, hands clasped in her lap. "We've found a place for you to live until the baby comes." She looked so relieved. "Jasia Boutacoff is an old friend of mine. We went to nurses' training together. She lives in the San Fernando Valley. I called and told her the situation. She said she'd be happy to have you come and stay with her. She'll take good care of you, Carolyn." She actually smiled as though things couldn't have worked out better. "What do you think?"

Dad's face darkened. "It doesn't matter what she thinks. It's what's best."

Mom covered her anger quickly. "You'll be much better off with Boots."

"Boots?"

"Jasia's nickname."

Dad's fingers stopped digging into the arm of his chair. "Charlie's car is yours now. I had it registered in your name." Dad glanced at Mom. "Boots gave you directions, didn't she?"

"Yes." Mom took a map and short note off the side table and held them out. "She said it would be easy to find. Her telephone number is at the bottom."

Carolyn took the map and directions in trembling fingers. They didn't have to say any more. She understood. They couldn't wait to get rid of her.

Dear Rosie,

I thought things might work out between Carolyn and her parents. Trip had softened, and I saw a desire on all sides to bridge the chasm. No matter the circumstances, this baby could have bound them together in love.

Trip and Hildemara sent Carolyn to Rev. Elias. The poor girl looked like something had broken inside her. She won't tell me a word of what the man said, but I can guess. I will never set foot in that church again as long as that sanctimonious hypocrite stands in the pulpit!

If that wasn't bad enough, this morning I learned Hildemara has sent Carolyn away. She and Trip decided Carolyn would be "better off" in Southern California among strangers than in Paxtown, "where she would be the brunt of cruel gossip." I asked Hildemara Rose if she cared more about what others think than how their daughter feels. She told me she knew what it felt like to be cast out, but that wasn't what she was doing to her daughter.

I am in Yosemite. I needed fresh air. I needed a walk in the mountains. My heart is broken, Rosie. I wanted to make my girl strong, not hard. . . .

WINDS GUSTED AS Carolyn drove over Altamont Pass. Spotting the Speedway sign, she remembered how much Chel had wanted to go to the concert. They'd both been too stoned to make it. Just as well. They missed the Hells Angels, the brawls, the fights and chaos. A steady stream of commuters headed back the way she had come, going west to Hayward and Oakland, maybe even as far as San Francisco.

August heat made the inside of Charlie's car feel soupy, even with the windows down. She turned south and kept on, pushing, wanting to speed, and then wondering why she was in such a hurry to get to a stranger's house. Before long, the Tehachapi Mountains loomed ahead, the Grapevine winding upward like a gray snake half-hidden by the inversion layer of smog and haze.

By the time she reached the San Fernando Valley, five o'clock traffic clogged the gray macadam arteries. She'd driven in traffic before, but not like this—six lanes, bumper to bumper, cars weaving, nosing in, taillights flashing red, horns honking if you hesitated a few seconds before making your decision. Adrenaline rushed in her veins. She developed a splitting headache. Her fingers ached from clutching the steering wheel. But she made the right exit and got on the right freeway.

It took forty-five minutes to go eleven miles, but she found her way to Canoga Park. She pulled into a shopping mall and bought her first meal of the day, Kentucky Fried Chicken. She didn't want to arrive on Jasia Boutacoff's doorstep hungry and begging for food. She reread the directions while she ate, and she had them memorized before she got back in the car and headed for Topanga Canyon.

The tan, two-story house with a Spanish red-tile roof stood at the end of a cul-de-sac, desert mountains looming behind. Carolyn parked, opened the trunk, took out her duffel bag, and hefted it onto her shoulder. The landscaping looked professional, trimmed juniper trees between boulders with river-rock ground cover. Two large terra-cotta pots with topiary privets and two Talavera pottery frogs sat on either side of the large mission-style door.

Carolyn had barely rung the bell when the door opened. "Jasia Boutacoff?"

"Call me Boots, honey." The tall, slender woman with gray-streaked black hair smiled warmly. She wore white slacks and a flowing purple tunic with a gold chain belt. "And you're Carolyn." She waved her in. "Come on in. It's hotter than Hades out here."

The air-conditioning hit Carolyn like a cold front, but she welcomed it after hours in hundred-degree heat. She smelled something wonderful cooking. The foyer had dark hardwood flooring, painted cabinets, Talavera sconces on the walls, and a large, frosted-glass Mexican star hanging from the ceiling. An archway opened into a dining room furnished with a painted country-style wood sunflower sideboard, a wrought-iron chandelier hanging over the painted table, and eight blue chairs.

"You must be exhausted after that long drive." She took Carolyn's bag. "I'll show you the way to your room. You can freshen up a bit, if you like, and join me in the living room." She led the way down a corridor without pausing for breath. "You

were six months old the last time I saw you. Your dad was changing your diapers." She laughed. "He gagged. Men are so helpless
sometimes."

Carolyn caught a glimpse of the huge Southwest-style living
room with a curved white fireplace and sliding-glass doors to
the backyard. Boots kept talking about Carolyn's dad and mom
as she walked down the hallway and opened a door into a large
bedroom, crossing the plush, tan carpeted floor. She put Carolyn's
duffel bag on the end of a four-poster queen-size bed with a crazy
quilt. Carolyn took in a Tuscan dresser on one side of the room,
marble-topped side tables, a comfortable chair with a stool near
the windows, a small table beside it with several books, one a Bible.
A watercolor of a field of sunflowers hung on one wall, an Italian
coastal town on the opposite.

Boots opened the big armoire. "You can put things in here,
or use the closet." She opened one of the sliding-mirror doors.
A dozen white silk hangers hung on the rod. "You have a private
bathroom." Boots leaned in and flicked on a light, revealing a
luxurious white marble bathroom with a big tub, separate shower,
and cubby room for the toilet. A thick terry-cloth robe lay over the
vanity chair. Mirrors lined the marble counter. Two sinks. Carolyn
had never seen anything so gorgeous.

"I'm so glad you're here, Carolyn. I'm looking forward to spending time with you. I want you to be comfortable. If you need
anything, you tell me. I want you to feel at home."

Overwhelmed, Carolyn burst into tears.

"Oh, sweetie." Boots held her close and rubbed her back.
"Don't worry. Everything is going to be fine. Things have a way
of working out the way God intends. I know this isn't your home,
but I'm going to do my best to make you feel as though it is.
You're not the first girl who's faced having a baby. You're not alone.
Believe me." She drew back and cupped Carolyn's face, leaning
down slightly to look into her eyes. "You're the daughter of one of
my oldest and dearest friends, and I promised Hildie I'd take good
care of you. Now I'm promising you."

She let go of Carolyn. "Why don't you freshen up and unpack? Come on in the living room when you're ready. We'll have a few minutes to talk before dinner is ready."

❉ ❉ ❉

Carolyn expected to hide out until the baby was born, but Boots dispelled that notion over a gourmet breakfast the next morning. "I've invited some friends over this afternoon. They've been a great comfort to me through some rough times. Kept me accountable. You're going to like them, and they're going to love you."

"I've never had many friends."

"Hildie said you had one that meant a lot to you." Boots looked at her.

What else had her mother told Boots?

"I can see what you're thinking. Your mother called me because she didn't want you among strangers. She knows my life hasn't been pristine. I was a party girl when we knew one another. She always walked the straight and narrow, but I dated every new intern who came to the hospital. No one was ever good enough for me, or so I thought. It took me a long time to realize I loved myself more than I'd ever loved anyone. And along the way, I found plenty of opportunities—and excuses—for getting drunk."

Boots lifted her glass of orange juice. "It never occurred to me I might become an alcoholic." She set the glass on the table. "No one sets out to bring that kind of misery into their life, and it takes more than willpower to stop." Completely relaxed, Boots smiled at Carolyn. "By the grace of God, someone dragged me to my first AA meeting. I heard about a higher power. I call Him Jesus. He's become the love of my life. And I made friends. You'll meet a few. I've been going to meetings ever since."

"The ladies who are coming today?"

"Only one, but none would claim to be perfect." She reached over and patted Carolyn's hand. "The thing is, we all struggle, some harder than others. Some of us make trouble for ourselves."

Carolyn hadn't just brought trouble on herself; she'd carried it home to her parents. She wondered how she'd support herself and her baby. She hadn't finished college, had no real job skills. Could she earn enough as a waitress or mall shopgirl to pay for a small apartment? What about doctor and hospital bills? If she kept her baby, she'd have to find work. She'd have to arrange day care. Would she end up raising her child in a ghetto neighborhood? There was always adoption, but Carolyn wanted to weep at the mere thought of handing her baby over to strangers, never to see her child again. Just thinking about all the decisions made her want to get drunk or high.

"I understand."

She hadn't realized she'd spoken the last aloud. Mortified, she closed her eyes.

"You don't have to figure everything out today, honey."

"I don't know if I can figure anything out."

"Take it one day at a time."

Carolyn wasn't used to trusting people, especially someone she'd known for so short a time, but she felt at ease with Boots. She felt safe. She'd been fighting temptation since she left the Clement Street house. If she'd had any money, she would've spent it on booze and drugs while living in the park. She had nothing then; she had nothing now, but the temptation hadn't lessened. Only the baby kept her straight.

"Can I go to an AA meeting with you sometime?"

"We'll go tonight."

❄ ❄ ❄

Mom called once a week. She'd ask Carolyn how she was feeling. "Fine." She'd ask how things were going with Boots. "Great." She'd ask if Carolyn needed anything. "No." Then she'd ask to speak with Boots.

Sometimes Dad got on the phone, but not often and never for long. Oma never called. She wrote letters, filling them with newsy

tidbits, what she had seen, what grew in her garden. She didn't ask
Carolyn if she'd made any decisions about the baby.

Dr. O'Connor, the husband of one of Boots's many friends,
told Carolyn the baby had a strong heartbeat. She'd gained ten
pounds in two months, largely due to Boots's great cooking. They
went on morning walks together before the heat trapped them
inside the house. Sometimes they went out again in the evening.
Boots insisted on "playing tourist" with her. They went to the Los
Angeles Zoo, Santa Monica Pier, La Brea Tar Pits, Malibu. When
Boots asked her if she'd like to go to Disneyland, Carolyn told
her about the trip with Oma. She no longer had to worry about
hurting Charlie's feelings.

They attended AA meetings twice a week. Carolyn listened, but
never talked. No one pressed her.

Boots tapped on her door early one morning. "We're going to
the beach before the crowds get there." She drove Topanga Canyon
Road like a NASCAR driver. They arrived at dawn. Joggers ran
along the water's edge.

"Come on." Boots got out and headed across the sand with
a basket and blanket. Dumping them, she kicked off her shoes
and continued on toward the waves lapping the beach. Carolyn
followed. Boots stopped at the edge of the wet sand. Hands on her
hips, she lifted her face and closed her eyes. "Listen to that. There's
something about the sound of the sea, isn't there? Soothing."

They walked along the beach together, not saying anything.
Boots didn't seem worried about the blanket. When they turned
back, she bent and scooped up a stick, twirling it in her hand like
a baton. "You're eating yourself up with guilt and worry, Carolyn,
and it's got to stop." She stopped and jabbed the stick into the
moist sand. "Write down every sin you've committed right here in
the sand. Let it all out." She walked up the beach onto dry sand,
spread the blanket, and sat. "Take your time!" she called out. She
lay back, arms beneath her head, and crossed her ankles.

Carolyn barely managed to write a few words before a wave
came and washed them away. She wrote more, and the waves came

in again, erasing her words. She wrote and wrote, and each time the sea came and swept away her confession. She didn't know how long she bent to the task before she finished. Her feet were numb from the cold water. She tossed the stick into the surf and watched it carried out. For the first time in weeks, her chest didn't feel like someone was sitting on it.

"Finished?" Boots called.

"For now."

Boots came down and stood next to her. "You can always come back." She smiled at her and then looked out at the sea. Surfers rode the small waves. "I listen to the sea and hear the Lord, Carolyn. Jesus said He came to save us, not condemn us. He took our sins upon Himself. He paid the price to set you free. God is like those waves, honey. He washes away your sins. He offers you the free gift of grace, the added bonus of the Holy Spirit dwelling in you, and eternal life as well. You have decisions to make, but the biggest one is what you're going to believe about Him. Ask Him in, and He'll take care of the rest."

They stood side by side looking out at the ocean. Carolyn felt a fluttering sensation—angel wings. She put her hands over her abdomen. Boots saw the movement and turned to her. "The quickening?" Carolyn laughed for the first time in months. It sounded odd to her ears. Boots laughed with her.

❄ ❄ ❄

Carolyn's heart pounded during AA meetings. She could feel the tension grow inside her. Sitting on her hands, she kept her head down, listening, soaking in the words.

One evening the silence lasted so long, she broke out in a sweat. She knew it was her turn to open up, but didn't know if she could speak a coherent sentence.

She took a breath and confessed she started drinking to deal with the stress of attending UCB. She drank more when her brother was sent to Vietnam, then started smoking pot with friends while protesting the war.

Everyone listened. No one judged her. Several came over to talk with her after the meeting, sharing similar stories.

"First time is usually hardest," Boots told her on the way home.

It took another month before she could talk about Charlie. She'd stayed drunk or stoned the year after he died. "I can only remember bits and pieces; most I'd rather forget. . . ." She cried when she told them about Chel.

Mom called again. Carolyn might not be able to talk with her mother, but Boots never had a problem. "She's filling out, has a nice basketball growing." Boots took pictures of Carolyn. When December rolled around, Mom and Dad sent money. So did Oma. Carolyn wrote and thanked them. Boots took her to the mall. As they wandered through the stores, Boots picked up a sweater. "Good godfrey! What a price!" She folded the sweater back onto the table. When she wasn't looking, Carolyn bought it for her.

Boots cried when she opened the box Christmas morning and found the red cashmere sweater. "You must have spent all your Christmas money on this."

"You like it, don't you?"

Boots put the sweater back in the box. "I love it, of course. But now you listen. Your mom and dad have been sending me money every month. I never asked for a penny, but they insisted. And then you go and buy this. I should take it back to the store."

"Please don't."

"Okay. I won't." She grinned, eyes brimming. "I'll throw you a shower instead."

Oma and Mom sent their regrets, inclement weather keeping them from making the long drive south. Oma had a bad cold, and Mom was keeping an eye on her.

A half-dozen friends of Boots showed up bearing gifts, most of which turned out to be for Carolyn and not the baby. A peach suit, white shell blouse, a pair of taupe heels and purse. "For job interviews." A jogging suit "to get back in shape after the baby." A classic camel-hair coat.

They couldn't have been kinder, though their expectation was clear: adoption was the best option. Only Boots gave her money to spend as she wanted.

Braxton Hicks contractions came often. Carolyn knew she didn't have much time left. She cried more now than she had during the earlier months, and she dreamed of sleeping in Golden Gate Park, lying on a sleeping bag beneath a black plastic lean-to. When she awakened, she reminded herself of Jesus speaking in that loving voice, His hand upon her, the tiny starlike flowers blooming in the grass, and dawn coming.

Mom finally asked the dreaded question. "Have you decided what to do?"

Carolyn noted her mother didn't ask what she *wanted* to do. Her eyes burned. She swallowed hard and wiped tears from her cheeks. "I guess." Give up her baby to someone else to rear. Everyone seemed to think that best, except Boots, who said things had a way of working out. Carolyn didn't see how. Had they worked out for Chel?

"You can stay with me as long as you want, Carolyn. You want to keep the baby, we'll work things out so you can."

Carolyn felt ashamed. Chel had paid for everything after they'd left Berkeley. She didn't want someone else paying her way now. It was just another way to run and hide from the real world. She had to grow up sometime, had to bear the consequences of her actions, no matter how painful. And wouldn't her baby be better off with someone else, someone less screwed up? someone who could offer a home and love? In three weeks, more or less, she'd give birth. She had to stop dreaming.

She called the adoption agency. They said they'd draw up papers. She cried all the way back to Boots's house.

Carolyn went out for a long walk alone the next morning. She had memorized the Serenity Prayer and said it over and over.

"A package came for you last night," Boots told her over

breakfast. "I forgot all about it when you came home so upset. I put it on your bed."

Boots had sliced open the cardboard box. Carolyn lifted out the big pink- and blue-papered box. When she opened the card, she recognized her mother's neat handwriting.

Dad and I hope this helps you make your decision. We love you.

They'd sent a baby car seat.

My dearest Carolyn,

I had a quiet Christmas with Bernhard, Elizabeth, and Eddie. I'm in Truckee now, enjoying snow-covered mountains, remembering the days I took long walks in the Alps with my friend, Rosie. She has been my faithful friend through all these years. She knows all my faults and failures and still loves me. May Boots prove such a friend to you.

I'm in no hurry to go home. All I do is sit alone in the cottage. Your mother is working long hours at the hospital. Your dad comes home and goes right to work building the retaining walls for the terraces he has planned. Rikka wants me to come to New York City in the spring. A gallery will be showing her work.

You and my first great-grandchild are in my constant

prayers. God grant you peace in whatever decision you make. I love you. That will never change. And I will love your child, too, no matter what happens.

    Life has its twists and turns, Carolyn. As for me, I am surrendering all to Jesus and trust Him to make it all straight in the end. Whatever you may think now, God promises to use everything that happens for His good purpose in making you into the woman He designed you to be. Just love Him. Lean on Him. Remember He loved you first and always. As do I.

Love,
Oma

❈ ❈ ❈

1971

Labor started in the middle of the night on February 6. Boots acted as Carolyn's coach. Boots washed the baby and wrapped her. The moment Carolyn held her newborn, she roused from exhaustion and wept with joy. She fell in love for the first time. Her daughter fit perfectly in her arms. Carolyn felt a tug at her breast as tiny fingers closed around her thumb. God had given her this child the night she had almost thrown her life into the sea. Tangible evidence of His grace.

Boots's eyes shone with tears over her surgical mask. "Well, you can't name her Charlie now, can you?"

"Her name is May Flower Dawn." She knew it sounded like a hippy name, but she didn't care. She couldn't call her the only other name that fit—Epiphany.

She'd conceived the baby the night before she saw Jesus, and she would always consider this child an undeserved gift from God.

❄ ❄ ❄

Mom called every few days to check on things. "Everything is ready." After a month, she lost patience. "It's time to come home, Carolyn. Boots has done enough."

May Flower Dawn slept most of the way. Carolyn stopped every couple of hours to nurse and change diapers. When she arrived home, Mom and Dad came outside. Oma came out of the cottage. Before Carolyn could get out of the car, her mother opened the passenger door and lifted May Flower Dawn from the car seat.

Her parents had turned Charlie's room into a nursery. They'd painted the walls pale green. Mom had hung airy white curtains. Dad had put up new pull-down shades and set up the white crib. Oma had bought the mobile with Disney characters. Dad had painted the bookcase white. Charlie's sci-fi books were gone and in their place, two stacks of diapers, Vaseline, baby powder, baby shampoo, bath soap, and some children's books.

May Flower Dawn still in her arms, Mom opened the closet. "Your grandmother has been sewing since she found out she has a great-granddaughter."

"So have you," Oma said from the doorway.

They had even bought a rocking chair. Mom sat in it. She laid May Flower Dawn on her lap. "She's beautiful." When May Flower Dawn started to whimper, Mom lifted her to her shoulder.

Carolyn stepped forward and reached out. "She's hungry."

Reluctantly, it seemed, Mom relinquished May Flower Dawn. Carolyn waited until her mother, father, and grandmother filed out of the bedroom before sitting on Charlie's bed to nurse her baby. She looked around the room again, taking in all the work her parents and Oma had done.

They might not love or want *her*, but Carolyn had no doubt they wanted May Flower Dawn.

CAROLYN SAT AT the dining room table, Dad at the head, Mom sitting opposite with May Flower Dawn in her arms again. While she cooed softly to Carolyn's baby, Dad did the talking. "It's not going to be a free ride. You'll have conditions to meet if you're going to live here." He folded his hands on the table. "We expect you to finish college and get your degree. And we expect you to work and pay rent."

Panic bubbled. "How?"

"You got yourself into this mess, and you're going to have to work your way out. Here's how things are going to be."

"You'll have two more months to rest and take care of the baby." Mom spoke without lifting her head. "By then, our little lady here will have had the most important benefits of nursing." When May Flower Dawn grasped Mom's thumb, Carolyn felt a twinge of jealousy. "I'll step in then."

"Step in?"

"Your mother is giving up her career in order to stay home and take care of your daughter."

"I didn't ask—"

"No, you didn't ask, but what did you think, Carolyn?" His eyes darkened in anger. "You could live off other people because you have a child?" His voice became tighter, harsher. "We can't take care of you for the rest of your life. You have to learn how to pay your way."

Mom raised her head. "Trip . . ."

Dad glanced at her and at the baby in her arms. His shoulders sagged. He looked back at Carolyn, his expression bleak. "We're not trying to punish you, Carolyn. We want to help you put your life back together. You need to finish school. Berkeley is out of the question, so we filled out the application for State College in Hayward. All you have to do is sign it. The college has an employment office. They'll help you find a job that will work into your school schedule."

Mom looked at her sadly. "It isn't going to be easy."

"Life isn't easy." Dad's mouth flattened. "We won't be around forever, picking up the pieces. You need a way to support yourself. Without an education, you're not going to get much of anything. We tried to tell you—"

Mom cleared her throat.

May Flower Dawn began to cry, a whimper at first, then louder, her little mouth opening and quivering as she wailed. Carolyn wanted to do the same thing. She started to stand. "Let me take her, Mom."

Mom stood, too, and shook her head. "She'll be fine. You and Dad need to talk." She took the baby into the back bedroom and closed the door, leaving Carolyn alone in the dining room with her father. He hadn't finished laying down the rules.

"You'll pay us rent. Not much, and not until you start working, but after that, we want eighty percent of whatever you make. It'll go for room and board and to repay the money we sent to Boots. And the hospital bill."

The full weight of what he expected fell on her like a load of bricks. How many years would it take to pay off her debts—ten?

twenty? May Flower Dawn would be grown and gone by then. She could hear her baby crying and wanted to go after her, wanted to grab hold of May Flower Dawn and run.

"Excuse me." Carolyn stood.

"Where are you going?"

"She's hungry."

She didn't tap at the bedroom door. She walked in. "She needs to nurse, Mom."

Mom smiled. "Sit here beside me and I'll give her to you."

Were there going to be conditions on everything now? Maybe there always had been. She hadn't understood the rules she had to follow to earn love. When Mom didn't rise from where she sat on the edge of the big double bed, Carolyn obeyed. Mom handed over May Flower Dawn, but didn't leave her alone.

Mom put her hand on Carolyn's knee. "I know you probably won't believe this right now, but Dad and I aren't doing this to ruin your life. We're not trying to make things even harder for you; we're trying to help you learn how to stand on your own two feet."

Carolyn looked into her mother's eyes and saw compassion. She also saw pain, and she knew she had caused it. "I know, Mom."

She also knew the price they asked: May Flower Dawn.

❋ ❋ ❋

What her parents demanded wasn't in writing. They didn't ask for her signature on any document. But it was a binding contract nonetheless, and Carolyn agonized over it. She could see no way out, nor did she feel she had the right to seek one. For the next six weeks, she pondered what she would have to do to make a way for herself and her daughter. If she went back to Boots, she would destroy a friendship that had weathered more than thirty years. She couldn't do that to her mother or to Boots.

So Carolyn signed the college application, put May Flower Dawn into the car seat, and drove into Hayward to hand-deliver it. Every course she had completed at UCB would count at State.

At least that was something, though she would still have two and a half years of coursework to complete while working part-time. If she went to school half-time, it would take her five years.

Could she do it? She spoke with the employment office. They assured her they would be able to find something for her when the semester began.

Time passed too quickly. She grasped every moment with May Flower Dawn, holding her, playing with her, watching her sleep. When Mom gave two weeks' notice at the hospital, Carolyn wept.

The first week of separation from May Flower Dawn proved agonizing. Her milk came in when she would have been feeding her, and the pain was excruciating. By the time she returned home, her mother had given May Flower Dawn formula, bathed her, changed her, and rocked her to sleep. Carolyn was left to take a warm shower and watch her milk flow down the drain.

She got a job in the library. She worked twenty-five hours a week, minimum wage. At the end of the month, she signed over her paycheck to her father. Dad had given her an accounting. Most of her check would go toward the hospital bill and Boots repayment, then toward room and board. Once the hospital bill and Boots had been taken care of, Carolyn could chip away at what she owed for tuition and books. He gave her twenty-five dollars to call her own. What she didn't spend on gas for Charlie's Impala went into a savings account.

Depressed, driven, Carolyn thought about drinking again. At least drunk she wouldn't feel the pain, the loneliness. Frightened by the craving, she found an AA meeting in Hayward. It helped to have friends who understood, a place where she could draw hope from others' experiences. But it took another hour out of her day, an hour she might have spent with May Flower Dawn.

Between classes, work, and AA meetings, Carolyn missed every milestone in May Flower Dawn's first year. Carolyn wasn't there when her baby daughter rolled over, learned to grasp a toy, sat up, or began to crawl. She didn't hear her say *Mama*. Mom and Dad began calling her daughter Dawn, and when she needed comfort or wanted something, she didn't reach out to Carolyn. She wanted Granny.

❄ ❄ ❄

1974

Finally growing weary of her library job, Carolyn used a portion of her savings to buy business attire and applied for part-time work as a receptionist in a real estate office owned by Myrna Wegeman, an attractive, ambitious overachiever, who hired her and started Carolyn at fifty cents more an hour than she'd been earning. Carolyn still had nights and Sundays free to study and attend AA meetings, but hardly any time at all with three-year-old Dawn. Mom and Dad didn't complain, and Dawn didn't miss her.

With a constant stream of new listings, Myrna handed Carolyn an expensive camera and sent her out to take pictures of properties. Carolyn studied the houses from every angle before shooting the pictures. Myrna couldn't have been more pleased with the results.

"I'm getting more calls on the properties you've shot than the ones I've done. You have a talent for this. Ever think about becoming a real estate agent?"

The more Carolyn did for Myrna, the more Myrna expected of her. When Myrna began asking her to oversee open houses on Sunday afternoons, Carolyn asked for double pay. Myrna reluctantly agreed.

This time, Carolyn ran into resistance at home. Mom balked at the idea of longer hours. "You're hardly ever home as it is."

Dad didn't like the idea either. "Your mother could use a break once in a while."

So could I! Carolyn wanted to say. She never had a day off, not that she dared ask for one. "I can take May Flower Dawn with me." The idea of having her daughter to herself for an entire afternoon excited her, but Mom nixed that idea.

"Maybe she should take Dawn with her, Hildie. Give Carolyn a chance to find out how hard it is to take care of a child."

Mom gave Dad a quelling look. "You make it sound like labor. I love taking care of Dawn. She's no bother at all!"

Dad gave up on Mom and directed his logic at Carolyn. "You've got plenty of time. You don't have to be in such a hurry. You're making good enough headway on your debts."

Carolyn realized they had no concerns over how much time she'd already lost with May Flower Dawn.

Oma came over early one Sunday before heading to church. She no longer attended church in Paxtown, but drove to a neighboring town. Mom had commented on it once. "Oma can't stand to be in the same building with Thelma Martin. Not that I blame her. But I'm not letting that gossip drive me away."

No one ever suggested Carolyn return. Certainly Rev. Elias never did.

Oma set her purse on the breakfast counter. "When was the last time you spent more than an hour with your daughter?"

"I don't have an hour, Oma. I have classes. I have to study. I have to work."

Oma watched Carolyn write notes. "Your mom and dad are doing what they think is right. They're doing the best they can for both you and May Flower Dawn."

Carolyn looked up from her textbook. "I know. I'm not complaining. It's just the way things are." Flipping the page in her text, she tried to refocus on her studies. "Sorry. I don't mean to ignore you, but I only have a couple of hours to study before I have to leave for an open house." She could feel Oma looking at her. How long since they had sat on the patio and had tea together?

"Maybe you should speak up about what you're feeling, Carolyn."

"Feeling?" Carolyn gave a bleak laugh. Speaking up wouldn't change anything. It would make things a hundred times worse! Oma didn't move. Frustrated, Carolyn stopped writing and looked at her. "And you don't have to say it. I already know. By the time I have a place of my own, Dawn won't be mine anymore."

"It's never been about possession."

"Maybe not, but that's the way it's turned out. And I'm losing ground with every day that passes." No matter how little time she spent with her child, she loved her. She longed to have her back in her arms. Why else did they think she worked so hard? She wanted her life back, a life that centered on May Flower Dawn.

Oma reached over and gripped her wrist, eyes flashing. "I took care of you when you were little more than a toddler. You *needed* me. Do you remember? But that didn't change the fact that your mother is still your mother!"

"Yes. I remember." Carolyn put her hand over Oma's. "But I learned to love you more, didn't I?"

Oma's eyes flickered. She had an odd expression on her face. Picking up her purse, she stood. "It never stopped you from loving her." She went quietly out the door.

Dear Rosie,

I see more clearly now how things I thought I did for good caused harm. Remember when I moved in with Hildemara when she was ill with consumption? I wanted to help, but ended up taking over. I became so attached to Carolyn, I didn't see the damage I did to my daughter.

Now I find myself watching Carolyn suffer as Hildemara must have. The girl is working so hard to put her life back together and earn love, all because Trip laid out a plan for her to "get back on her feet" and "fly right." They want to help, just as I did. But these conditions have left no time for Carolyn to be with her child, no time to be part of the family. I hardly ever see Carolyn anymore. We barely have time to exchange a greeting, let alone sit under the arbor and have a cup of tea. How can I encourage her? I have no answers.

I have never seen Hildemara so happy (other than her complaints that Carolyn no longer attends church). I understand her happiness because I felt the same when I took care of Carolyn. I felt the loss of my daughter's affections far less when I could freely pour my love out on my granddaughter. And there is the dilemma!

Did I have the right to usurp Hildemara in Carolyn's affections as I now see her doing with May Flower Dawn? Hildemara is in her glory. She does all the things a mother longs to do for her child. Of course, Carolyn does not complain about anything. She has always been reticent about sharing her feelings. Yesterday she surprised me and said her mother never had time for her, but all the time in the world for May Flower Dawn. She didn't say it with bitterness, but resignation.

I've been pondering Carolyn's words ever since. I wonder if Hildemara feels the same about me. . . .

19

1976

Time moved too quickly. Carolyn's mother had enrolled Dawn in nursery school and stayed as a volunteer. Carolyn pushed harder than ever as she went into her senior year of college. Myrna urged Carolyn to study for a real estate license. "I have more clients than I can handle, and you've already learned how to write proposals and put the paperwork together." Myrna had seen to that. "You'd make a lot more money than you do as my receptionist."

Adding another goal chewed into what little time Carolyn had left. She wished she could quit college, but Dad wouldn't hear of it. "Real estate markets go up and down. A college degree lasts forever." The last few months proved to be the most taxing, and then she got the word she had made it. She told Dad, knowing he would care more than Mom. Only one hitch.

"What do you mean you're not going through the graduation ceremony?"

Carolyn shrugged it off. "It's not important. I'll get my diploma in the mail."

"Don't you think you owe it to us to walk across that stage?"

She wanted to remind him she had already given him and Mom everything he demanded—and the one thing that mattered most to her, May Flower Dawn. "The test for my real estate license is on the same day, Dad. I have more chance of making a living at real estate than as an officer manager." She'd already checked. It was still a man's world. All her business degree would get her was a menial job in a big corporation and low starting pay. She didn't have any more time to waste.

"Doesn't it matter to you, Carolyn?" Her father looked troubled. "You've worked so hard. You should be proud. I'd think you'd want to wear that cap and gown and have the whole world see you get your diploma."

The whole world? Who was he kidding? Carolyn felt a sudden rush of anger. "It mattered more to you than it ever mattered to me."

"Why didn't you say something?"

"And where would I've been if I had? I'd have done *anything* to stay off the streets. I've done everything you and Mom asked of me, and you're still not satisfied."

Dad winced as though she'd slapped him across the face. She had to clench her teeth before she lied and retracted every word.

❄   ❄   ❄

Real estate license in hand, Carolyn gave Myrna Wegeman notice. "You're quitting?" Myrna couldn't believe it. "After all I've done for you?"

Carolyn thanked her. "You've taught me more about business than all my classes put together. You're the one who believed in me and made me feel I could do so much more." She wanted to work in the valley, close to May Flower Dawn. She wanted time with her daughter.

Myrna wasn't mollified. "You owe me for the opportunities I've given you!"

Carolyn had had enough. She didn't want to hear how much

she owed Myrna—or anyone else. She'd been working on her debts for five years! "I'm sorry you feel that way. I hoped we could part as friends." Forget the two weeks' notice. She headed for the door.

Myrna came out from behind her desk and called out to her to wait a minute. "Can't we talk about this?" Carolyn didn't even look back as she went out the door and closed it firmly behind her.

She'd already lined up a job in a real estate office in Paxtown. Real estate boomed over the East Bay hills, too, and Ross Harper had been willing to hire her, despite having been warned by others of her less-than-pristine reputation. He'd heard of Myrna Wegeman. "If you survived three years with that tiger, working with me is going to be a piece of cake."

She no longer had to get up at the crack of dawn to commute to the Bay Area. She no longer had night classes. She didn't have to spend every spare minute studying and writing papers. She could breathe a little, as long as she scoured the valley in search of people willing to list property with a young, untried real estate agent. And then she had to promote those properties to other agents and show the houses.

America's bicentennial came, and Carolyn managed enough time off to attend the fireworks and celebration at the fairgrounds. Five-year-old May Flower Dawn was frightened by the explosions and bright, showering lights. When Carolyn tried to snuggle her close, she cried harder. Straining away, Dawn called out for "Granny" and wouldn't be calmed until sitting on Mom's lap.

A week later, Carolyn sold her first listing and used every bit of her commission to pay off the last of the debt she owed her father and mother. She felt a moment of ecstasy when she handed Dad the check.

"Against all odds." His eyes glistened with tears. "You did it, Carolyn." He smiled broadly. "I'm proud of you."

She had never expected those words to come out of his mouth, not in a million years. Embarrassed, she stammered. "I have some buyers interested in another listing. If all goes well, I'll have enough to move out on my own." She glanced toward the living room, where May Flower Dawn played with Barbie dolls while Mom read a story.

Mom left the book on the table and came through the foyer. "What are you two talking about?"

Dad showed her the check. "She's debt-free."

Mom held the check in both hands and stared at it. No congratulations were forthcoming. Carolyn stood a little straighter. "I was telling Dad if I make another sale, I'll be moving out with May Flower Dawn."

"Moving out?" Mom raised her head, her face paling.

"She won't be going far." Dad seemed oblivious. "She works for Ross. Remember? It's not like she'd be moving to the San Fernando Valley."

Dad didn't seem to notice Mom's pained glance back at the child playing on the living room rug. Carolyn did, and she understood only too well. Her mother wasn't worried about losing her. She just didn't want to lose May Flower Dawn.

❄ ❄ ❄

When Carolyn came home the next afternoon after showing houses all morning to prospective buyers, her mother and father said they wanted to talk with her. Mom's red-rimmed eyes warned her something was wrong. "Where's May Flower Dawn?"

"She's fine." Mom wiped her cheek. "She's at Sandy's house."

"Sandy?"

"Her best friend from nursery school. They live on First Street."

"Nice family," Dad added. "They go to our church."

Carolyn knew less than nothing about May Flower Dawn's classmates. That would soon change. She clasped her hands tightly in her lap. "You wanted to talk to me about something?"

He smiled. "Actually, we wanted to give you something." He slid a bankbook across the table. When she didn't touch it, he nodded at it. "Go ahead. Take a look. It's yours."

She took it and wondered what catch her parents had attached to this. She put it back on the table and pushed it away. "I don't need a loan. I just wrote an offer on a house today. If it goes through, I'll receive a good commission. I've had my eye on an American bungalow out on Vineyard Avenue—"

Mom cut her off. "It's not a loan, Carolyn. It's yours."

"Every penny of it." Dad pushed the bankbook back to her. "It's every dollar of the rent money you've given us since you came home."

She stared at them. She didn't know whether to believe they could extend such kindness or pull defensive armor around herself. "I don't understand."

Dad leaned forward. "We knew you'd need a nest egg, Carolyn, something to give you a good start when you finished school. So we've been setting aside the rent money from the beginning."

Carolyn looked at her mother and saw a war of emotions. Did she understand this gift would become the means to take May Flower Dawn away from her? Mom's sad smile hinted she did; then her words confirmed it. "You should have enough to put a down payment on that bungalow you want."

"If I can talk them into selling, I will." Carolyn took the bankbook with trembling fingers. "Thank you."

Carolyn felt no qualms about embracing her father or soaking his shirt with tears. Hugging her mother proved more difficult. As soon as Carolyn put her arms around her, Mom stiffened and turned her face. Hurt, Carolyn took the hint and withdrew. Her mother's eyes filled with pain. She took Carolyn's hand, patting it. "You'll do fine."

❄ ❄ ❄

Carolyn wasted no time. She went to the Zeiglers, who owned the house she liked, and asked if they might be interested in selling. She expected resistance, but they surprised her and agreed. They had been thinking about selling for over a year. "Our daughter would like us to move back to Ohio and live with her family. She has a big house on a lake, with a granny unit."

Everything moved quickly. Mrs. Zeigler called Carolyn and asked if she would be interested in buying some of their furniture. "We won't have room for most of our things." The only thing they wanted to take east was their bedroom set, a gift to each other on their fortieth wedding anniversary. Carolyn bought their sofa, wing chairs, bookshelves, a dining room set, a large mahogany coffee table, two standing tulip lamps, and the brass fire screen and utensils. She had made another sale and went out to find something special for May Flower Dawn. She purchased a French provincial twin canopy bed, white dresser, desk, and two matching side tables.

Carolyn used every spare moment to get the house ready for May Flower Dawn. She washed walls and painted; put up new drapes and sheers; had the wood floors in the living room sanded, restained, and sealed; and bought an imitation Persian rug. She added wall-to-wall carpeting in the bedrooms. Mom had told her May Flower Dawn's favorite colors. She painted the walls of her daughter's bedroom pink with white trim, bought pink sheets and blankets and a purple comforter set with pillow shams. She hung white lace curtains and bought new Barbie and Ken dolls with half a dozen changes of clothes.

Carolyn worked far into the night every night, wanting everything to be perfect before her daughter moved in. By the end of her first month of home ownership, she was ready. "Everything's been done, Mom. I want to make things as easy as possible for both of you. Do you want to bring May Flower Dawn, or shall I come and get her?"

"Dad and I will bring her to you. We'd like to see what you've done to the place."

When her parents arrived, Carolyn watched her daughter's face, hoping to see some hint of pleasure. May Flower Dawn looked scared. She clutched her grandmother's hand and avoided Carolyn's eyes. Mom had a forced smile plastered to her face. She talked in an overbright voice, pointing out what a nice house Dawn would be living in. "What a lovely bedroom. Your mother painted it your favorite colors, honey."

"I don't want to live here, Granny." May Flower Dawn spoke in a low voice.

"This is your home now, Dawn."

"I want to stay with you and Papa."

Every word stabbed Carolyn's heart. Mom was clearly grief torn. Dad looked grim and somewhat irritated. "We'd better go, Hildie. Now."

"Just give me a minute with her."

Carolyn wanted to scream. *You've had her for five years, and I've given you weeks to prepare her!* Pushing the pain and anger down, she quietly left them alone and went outside with Dad. He gazed back toward the house. "Don't expect Dawn to adjust overnight, Carolyn."

She tried to be fair. "I suppose it's going to be difficult for Mom, too."

"You have no idea."

Mom came outside alone, eyes streaming tears. "If you need us, just call." She slipped quickly into the car and covered her face, shoulders shaking. Carolyn watched them drive away before she went back into the house. She found May Flower Dawn curled up and crying on her new bed.

Sitting on the edge, Carolyn put her hand on her daughter's shoulder. "I love you, too, you know."

"Why can't I live with Granny and Papa?"

"Because I'm your mother. You belong with me."

She peered up at Carolyn, eyes red-rimmed, face awash with tears. "You've never wanted me before."

Carolyn drew in a sharp breath of pain. "That's not true, May Flower Dawn. I've always wanted you, from the first moment I knew you were on the way. Everything I've done has been for you." She looked into her daughter's blue eyes and knew she didn't believe her.

"My name is *Dawn*."

"Your name is May Flower Dawn Arundel. Dawn is your middle name."

Her daughter's lip quivered. "The *Mayflower* was a ship."

"You weren't named after a ship."

"Papa said it's a hippy name."

Carolyn supposed that was how her father and mother might perceive it. She felt wounded by the reminder of their condemnation. "May . . . Flower . . . Dawn. Three separate words, each with precious meaning."

Her daughter blinked and stared at her face. "I like the name Dawn."

Should she explain how she had come up with the name? Perhaps it was better not to look back. Other questions might come up, like who her father was. "All right. Dawn, it is."

"Can I see Granny and Papa?"

"Of course." She tried not to let the hurt show. "It's not like we've moved to the other side of the moon."

Even that assurance didn't ease things for more than a little while. Carolyn heard her daughter crying that night—and every night that followed. Dawn didn't like anything she cooked. When she asked her daughter what she did like, she shrugged. Carolyn knew it wasn't the food that mattered, but the hands that prepared it.

Other more serious problems quickly developed.

Carolyn had to pick up Dawn from school and keep her at the office for the afternoon. A kindergartner didn't have homework to keep her occupied, and coloring didn't hold May Flower Dawn's interest for long. Her daughter wandered and got in the way. When she accidentally knocked a stack of files off Ross's desk, he called Carolyn into his office.

"You're going to have to make other arrangements for your daughter, Carolyn. I can't have her in here."

Carolyn remembered coming home to an empty house when she was May Flower Dawn's age. She remembered gravitating to

Dock's warm welcome and how that had turned out. "She just needs a little more time to adjust, Ross."

"No. A child shouldn't be cooped up in an office all afternoon. She should be outside playing with friends."

Stung, Carolyn asked for a few days to work things out. She called her grandmother. "Oma, I don't know what to do."

"Of course you do. Ask your mother to babysit."

"I'd be handing May Flower Dawn back to her."

"No. You'd be sharing her."

Carolyn wanted to weep. Sharing? Over the past five years, how much time had Mom allowed with her daughter? "You don't understand."

"I understand better than you do, Carolyn." She sounded sad and tired. "Don't make it a tug-of-war."

When Carolyn hung up, she put her head in her hands and wept. Gulping down sobs, she looked up and saw May Flower Dawn standing in the doorway, frightened and upset. Carolyn wiped her face. "It's okay. You're going to get what you want."

Running up the white flag, Carolyn called her mother. She could hear Mom's relief and pleasure. "Of course! I can pick her up after school. She can stay here until you're off work. You can drop her off anytime you need to show houses. I'd love to have her!"

She hadn't had May Flower Dawn back for a month before she lost her again.

Life went more smoothly after that. At least Mom and Dawn were happy.

1977

It had been seven years since Carolyn left San Francisco and came home. Seven years of demolishing the old and constructing her new life. She'd hoped it would become easier with time. She hoped people would forget her past and allow her to raise her head without feeling censorious eyes upon her.

With only one bank in town, Carolyn often saw someone who knew her past. Today, that person just happened to be Thelma Martin. She came in shortly after Carolyn got in line to wait for a teller. She could feel Thelma's eyes boring into the back of her head. They hadn't spoken since Carolyn left the dentist's office. Carolyn's muscles clenched tight as she focused on not turning around. The woman had spread more poison in Paxtown than anyone, and she still seemed to delight in dredging up Carolyn's history for anyone curious enough to listen.

A teller opened up, and Carolyn made a beeline to her window to make her deposit. "Can I do anything else for you, Miss Arundel?"

Carolyn said no thank you, stuffed her checkbook into her shoulder bag, and headed quickly for the door. She barreled right into someone standing just outside. The man steadied her.

"I'm so sorry." She stepped back from his touch, face hot. "Excuse me."

"Carolyn?"

Flustered, she looked up. She hadn't seen this tall, broad-shouldered, red-haired stranger around town, but he looked familiar. In the split second she looked into his green eyes, her pulse shot up. She tried to place him. Had she slept with him in Haight-Ashbury? She hoped not, but the memories of those awful days came fresh to mind every time she saw Thelma Martin's condemning glare.

"Mitch Hastings." He smiled at her. "Remember me now? Your brother and I rode bikes together, until he got a red Impala."

She had driven the Impala until Dad had said it wasn't safe to drive anymore. She hated seeing it towed away, hated even more the payments for another used car.

When she didn't say anything, he went on. "We played football together in high school. I played offensive lineman so he could score all those touchdowns."

His smile made Carolyn's insides quiver strangely. That alone made her want to run. She glanced away and saw Thelma Martin heading straight for the door. "Nice to see you again, Mitch." She didn't even extend her hand. "I have to run." She stepped around him and walked quickly toward her car.

"Wait a minute." He caught up with her easily and fell into step beside her. "What's your hurry?"

"I have to get back to work."

"Can I call you?"

"Sorry." She got into her car. If he kept standing where he was, she'd run over his toes. She glanced at him as she backed out. Cranking the wheel, she shot out of the parking lot. She glanced in her rearview mirror. Mitch stood, hands on his hips, looking bemused. He turned his attention to Thelma Martin when she came up to him and extended her hand. No doubt Thelma Martin would feel it her civic duty to warn Mitch off having anything to do with the town slut.

The telephone rang within minutes of her return to Ross Harper's agency. His wife, Candace, answered. "Yes, she is. She just walked in the door. One moment please." She smiled at Carolyn. "Call on line two. He has a nice voice."

"Carolyn Arundel. How can I help you?"

"You can go with me to my class reunion tonight." Mitch Hastings didn't waste time.

She couldn't imagine anything worse than a Paxtown class reunion—it didn't matter what year. "No, thank you."

"I know it's short notice. If I'd known you were back in town, I would've gotten in touch sooner." He chuckled. "It was providential we ran into one another."

Clearly, Thelma had given him an earful about her past. He wasn't the first eager beaver wanting to go out with her and see how far he could get on a first date. Hence, she never went out. "I wasn't in your class."

"We're out of high school. The age difference doesn't matter anymore."

Meaning what? She'd been jailbait when she had a crush on him? "Try someone else." She hung up.

When she picked up May Flower Dawn that afternoon, her mother told her Mitch Hastings had been there for a visit. "He was a sight for sore eyes. I haven't seen him in years." She looked pleased and speculative. "He said he saw you in town."

"We bumped into one another."

"Did he tell you he's a certified financial planner now?"

"We had about two seconds to exchange greetings, Mom. I had to get back to work."

"He told Dawn stories about Charlie and had us all laughing. He has a place up north of Healdsburg; Alexander Valley, I think he said. He's in town for the class reunion. He said he asked you to go with him, but you said no. If you'd like to change your mind, he left his number. He's staying at the Paxtown Hotel. We can keep Dawn for the night. . . ."

"No, thanks."

"I always liked Mitch. He's a solid young man, Carolyn. Why don't you go? All you do is work. It wouldn't hurt to have some fun once in a while."

Carolyn had to bite her tongue to keep from telling her mother Thelma Martin had gotten to him first and poisoned the water. And how did anyone know what Mitch Hastings was? Mom just said she hadn't seen him in years. Carolyn didn't feel safe with what he'd stirred in her in less than a minute. "I don't need any more complications in my life." She preferred loneliness to feeling used. Several of her brother's friends still lived in the valley. When they called her out of the blue, she knew why. She could hear it in the seductive tones they used, the way they promised her a good time. Saying no hadn't changed her reputation. What man wants to admit he's been shot down? Better to smile and let people believe things went exactly as people like Thelma Martin expected. She didn't go out with anyone. She didn't trust herself where men were concerned. All she had to do was look back. Why open the door to more hurt?

Mitch called the office again on Monday. "How about lunch?"

"I thought you just came for the reunion."

"I decided to stay a few extra days."

Carolyn's body responded to the warmth in his voice, which made her more wary. "Well, enjoy yourself. I'm busy."

"You have to eat sometime."

"I brought a sandwich."

Ross turned and looked at her, brows raised. Thankfully, another line rang, distracting him. Candace had gone on break and wasn't around to answer.

Mitch cleared his throat softly. "Did I do or say something to offend you, Carolyn?"

"No. It isn't that." When another line started ringing, Ross glanced at her. "Sorry, but I have another line coming in. Can't talk." She hung up and hoped he'd take the hint and leave her alone.

Someone wanted to see a house in Paxtown Heights. "I can show you the property now, if you'd like." She jotted down the prospective buyer's address, grabbed her keys, and headed for the door. She didn't return until midafternoon.

Ross nodded toward her desk. "Mitch Hastings called you back. He wants to see one of your properties out on Foothill Road."

She threw her shoulder bag into the bottom drawer of her desk and kicked it shut. "Why don't you take him?"

He grinned all too knowingly. "He didn't ask for me."

"He isn't interested in buying that house, Ross. He already has a place up in Sonoma County somewhere."

He leaned back in his swivel chair. "So?"

Candace decided to join the conversation. "People have been known to buy more than one house."

"Nothing ventured, nothing gained." Ross smiled. "Go talk to him."

Fuming, Carolyn got her purse out of the drawer and left again. On the way to the hotel, she tried to rehearse what to say. Heart pounding, she waited while the clerk called and told him, "A lady is in the lobby, Mr. Hastings." He listened and hung up. "He said he'll be right down."

When Mitch appeared, she opened her mouth, but he put his hand at the small of her back and guided her toward the dining room, not the front door. She dug in her heels. "I was told you wanted to see a house out in the foothills."

"Ross said you hadn't had a chance to eat before you went out to show the other place."

"I'm not hungry."

"Yes, you are. Your stomach just growled."

The host looked as though he expected them. "Right this way." He led them to a small private table overlooking the gardens.

Mitch held her chair. "We can talk over lunch."

She couldn't refuse without making a scene. Accepting the

proffered menu, she pretended to read it. "So what would you like to know about the house?"

"Give it a rest."

Too nervous to eat, she ordered a small salad. Mitch ordered a steak. Her palms sweated when he looked at her over the table, green eyes glowing. She figured it was time to lay out the ground rules. "I don't go out with clients."

"No problem."

"And I don't like games."

"No game intended. I couldn't think of any other way to get you to go out with me."

"You might not be so interested if you knew the facts."

"So tell me."

Okay. Better now than later, when it would hurt more. "While Charlie was being a hero in Vietnam, I was burning my bra, smoking pot, and protesting the war in Berkeley, not that it did any good. The day my parents got the news Charlie had been killed, I took off for Haight-Ashbury. Everything you've heard goes on there? I did it all. I don't even remember how many guys I slept with. I was too stoned to care. When my best friend died of a heroin overdose, I left the commune and lived in Golden Gate Park. I slept in public restrooms, on park benches, and under bushes. I ate out of garbage cans. You met my daughter, May Flower Dawn. How'd I get her? I was cold one night. A stranger offered to share his sleeping bag. My baby is the only thing about my life I *don't* regret."

She tossed her napkin on the table.

Mitch caught her wrist before she could get up. "Past history, Carolyn. We all have regrets."

"Regrets? That's what you call it? Let go!"

"Not unless you give me equal time."

She held her breath, afraid he could feel the pulse in her wrist. "Please let go of me." His fingers loosened enough for her to slip free.

His mouth curved tenderly. "Please don't run." He managed

to sum up his life in less than two minutes. After a minor football injury put him on the bench, he quit college and joined the Marine Corps. "Maybe Charlie got the idea from me. Neither one of us knew what we wanted out of life other than *more*. I got tired of drinking beer, chasing girls, and playing football." He thought joining a cause would give his life purpose. It did, for a while. "I was in the jungle when Charlie was killed in Hue. I did two tours of duty before getting out, then went back to college. I finished at Ohio State with a business degree, then found a good job in Miami." When his father and stepmother were killed in a car accident in Key West, he inherited their home in Vero Beach. "I sold in a seller's market, invested the money, and took off on my motorcycle to see America."

Carolyn relaxed enough to eat. "What brought you back to California?"

He studied her for a long moment as though debating with himself before answering. "I'm a Californian at heart. Every place else seemed a little too tame. Healdsburg reminded me of Paxtown twenty years ago. I bought a ranch house on twenty acres in Alexander Valley, planted a vineyard, and went to work for a wealth management firm." He laughed. "They were impressed with my portfolio." The day he came to Paxtown, he went to visit Charlie's grave. He talked about Charlie after that, the fun they'd had riding bikes, hiking the foothills, playing football, cruising Main, and honking at girls. He made Carolyn laugh, something she hadn't done in a long time.

His gaze caressed her face. She tried to ignore the strong attraction. He smiled as though he knew exactly what she was feeling. Heart hammering, she glanced at her wristwatch. Gasping, she pushed her chair back. "I have an appointment." She grabbed her purse. "I'm sorry to eat and run, Mitch. Thank you for the lunch and for the journey back in time to more innocent days."

"Wait." He signed the check hastily and rose. "I'll walk you to your car." He took her hand as they went out the door. "How about dinner and a movie this evening?"

She pulled her hand free. "I can't."

"May Flower Dawn is welcome to come along."

She fumbled the key into her car door. "It's been nice, Mitch, but . . ."

Mitch turned her around. "Look at me, Carolyn." She saw the strength in his face, the confident man he had become. Again, she felt the jolt of attraction between them.

"You asked what brought me back to California. *You* did. I've been in love with you since I was fifteen." He gave a self-deprecating laugh. "You were eleven. Charlie didn't know then. He figured it out when you were in ninth grade. I dropped a class just so I could be in a study hall with you."

"Mitch . . ."

He slid his fingers into her hair, his eyes never leaving hers. "The thing is, I never got over you. I left for Ohio figuring that was it, I'd never see you again. And then I decided to come back and find out what happened to you." When he leaned down, she thought he meant to kiss her. She caught her breath. He stopped just short. "Just dinner. Okay? That's all I'm asking for right now." His breath caressed her face. "Say yes."

"Yes."

"Thank God." His hand slid down her neck, across her shoulder, and away. When he smiled, his eyes lit up and glowed with warmth. "Let's go someplace quiet where we can talk."

"Why don't you come to my place, and I'll fix dinner?" The moment the words escaped her lips, she couldn't believe she'd suggested it. What was she thinking? Worse, what might he think?

"Perfect. What time?"

Short of withdrawing the invitation, what could she say now? "Six thirty?"

He opened her car door. "I'll be there."

She made it to her appointment on time. When she drove out to pick up May Flower Dawn, Mom asked if she wanted a cup of tea before going home. Her mother looked surprised and pleased when she said yes. Carolyn had always had trouble talking with her mother, but today she felt like giving it a try. They sat in the living room while May Flower Dawn picked up her Barbies and put them back in her room. She never touched the dolls Carolyn bought.

"Have you heard from Mitch?" Mom sipped her tea.

"He called the office and asked to see a house."

"Is he planning to move back to Paxtown?"

"No. It was a hijacking."

Her mother laughed. "I guess he's not a man to take no for an answer." A frown flickered across her face, and Carolyn wondered what she might be thinking. She didn't want to give her mother any wrong ideas.

"We talked a lot about Charlie. I asked him over for dinner this evening."

"Why don't you let Dawn spend the night here?"

"I wouldn't want to give Mitch the wrong idea."

Setting her cup down, her mother looked at her. "I'm sure his intentions are honorable, Carolyn. If not, you *can* say no."

Carolyn couldn't help but laugh. "*Honorable.* I don't know what that means these days."

Her mother frowned, clearly troubled. "He was Charlie's best friend, Carolyn. He misses your brother. He probably just wants a quiet evening to talk with someone who loved him as much as he did."

If only that was all there was to it. She didn't want to say too much and have her mother speculating on what they might do, other than talk about Charlie.

Mom chuckled as she sipped her tea again. "Dawn was just telling me a while ago she'd like to ride the bus to school just once. If she stayed overnight, she could ride to school tomorrow."

"I don't know, Mom."

"Please!" May Flower Dawn spoke up from the foyer.

Her daughter seldom asked for anything from her. How could Carolyn say no?

❄ ❄ ❄

Home and alone, Carolyn decided to call the whole evening off. She phoned the Paxtown Hotel and asked to be put through to Mitch's room. The telephone rang ten times before the clerk came back on the line and said he was sorry, but Mr. Hastings seemed to be out for the afternoon. In a panic, Carolyn rummaged through her refrigerator, wondering what to fix for dinner. She threw together a meat loaf, put two potatoes in to bake, and made a tossed salad. She'd just finished setting the table when she heard a motorcycle out front. Her pulse rocketed. Her heart would have gone into orbit if it hadn't been encased in her chest.

The doorbell rang. Swiping the perspiration from her palms, Carolyn fixed a smile on her face and opened the door. "Hi, Mitch. Come on in." Her voice sounded so chipper, so high school. Mitch looked entirely too handsome in a black leather bomber jacket, casual blue henley shirt, black leather belt, Levi's, and boots. He held a bottle of red wine in one hand and a bouquet of lilies in the other. Swallowing hard, she opened the door wider and waved him in. "Can I take your coat?"

"Better take the wine and flowers first."

She blushed. "Of course."

As soon as his hands were free, Mitch stripped off his jacket, tossed it on the sofa, and followed her into the kitchen. "Something smells good."

"Does it?" She rattled off the menu. "Sorry. Nothing fancy."

"Got a corkscrew? I'll open the wine."

She fingered through her utensil drawer until she found a can opener that included one. "Here you go." His fingers brushed hers, and she dropped it. "Sorry." She stooped to pick it up and put it on the counter. Did he have to watch her like that? Her heart kept knocking wildly. She arranged the lilies in a vase and took it back into the dining room. She took a wineglass from the built-in china cabinet and put it on the table.

"Only one glass?"

"I'm a recovering alcoholic. An ex-pothead."

He grimaced. "Sorry."

"I'll try not to drool while you enjoy it." She tried to make it sound like a joke, but the words came out flat. "Dinner won't be ready for another forty-five minutes. Why don't we sit in the living room?" She waved toward the sofa, where he'd tossed his jacket. Mitch sat and watched her. Tense, she picked up his leather jacket and then wondered what to do with it. She should hang it up, but she didn't have a hall tree. She thought of her bedroom and discarded that idea. Giving up, she folded it over the sofa again.

She sat in one of the wing chairs, back stiff, hands clasped in her lap. "So. What shall we talk about?"

"You want to tell me why you're so nervous?"

"I've never invited a man over for dinner before." She smoothed her skirt over her knees. "You want to talk about Charlie?"

"Is May Flower Dawn going to join us?"

"Nope. She's spending the night with my parents." She felt her face flame up to her hairline as she considered how he might take that news. "It wasn't my idea."

His mouth tipped ruefully. "I'm sure it wasn't. I'll bet it was you calling my room this afternoon, trying to call the whole evening off."

So he had been there. "Why didn't you answer?"

"Why do you think?"

The look in his eyes didn't give her any room for speculation. Her mind flashed images of other men who had wanted her. Dock popped into her head, first. As she fled thoughts of him, Ash emerged from the pit, beautiful, charismatic, and on a power trip. More pain. More shame. How many others had she slept with who wanted her body, but cared as little about her as they did about the weather? She'd become the wasteland after the hurricane, the refuse washed up onshore, the broken trees, the crushed houses. And now, Mitch Hastings, Charlie's best friend, sat on a secondhand sofa in her living room, eyes full of a consuming fire, asking her what she thought.

She put her hands on the arms of the chair and pushed herself up. "I'm not much of a hostess. I didn't even think to offer you something to drink. I have Coke, 7UP, iced tea, lemonade, well water. Or you can start on the wine you brought."

"Nothing, thanks."

She sank into the chair again. Now what? She sought desperately for something to say. She dredged down into the darkness and came up empty. Thankfully, Mitch came to her rescue.

"You mentioned Charlie. We wrote letters back and forth after we left high school, kept up the correspondence when he went into the military. He wrote about you."

"I'll bet."

"He loved you, Carolyn. He worried about you."

She pressed her back against the chair and lifted one shoulder. "His dumb, screwed-up sister gone hippy." More cause for grief. "Mom and Dad said I made him ashamed."

"He never told me he was ashamed of you. He said you were trying to stop the war. He said you wanted to be his savior. He worried about your relationship with Rachel Altman. She seemed to have a lot of influence on you."

She bristled. "Charlie only met her once."

"Yeah, and it was that one meeting that made him worry. Apparently, she came into his bedroom in the middle of the night."

She blushed. "I know. She told me after the fact."

"He beat himself up over what happened. He said she was totally screwed up, and he took advantage."

Carolyn gave a soft laugh. "I think it was the other way around, Mitch."

"Whatever the case, Charlie liked her. A lot. He said there was something about her . . ."

"Chel sang a siren song." Like Janis Joplin, her idol, who died of a drug overdose less than a year after she did.

"They exchanged letters. He planned to look her up when he came home."

"Did he?" And now both of them were dead. She wanted Mitch

to get things straight. "No one can blame Chel for the things I did, Mitch. Some people are born into a mess. Some people find ways to mess up their own lives. It's the one thing at which I've always excelled."

"You put your life back together, Carolyn. That takes courage."

Mitch deftly turned the conversation to other things, managing to make the mundane interesting. She asked about his travels. He talked about riding cross-country on his Harley, interesting people he'd met in diners and campgrounds, sights he'd seen. Carolyn relaxed and enjoyed listening to him. When the timer went off, she put the food on the table. She poured him a glass of wine and set the bottle down before taking her seat across from him. He asked if it would be all right if he said grace. Surprised, she said please, and when he finished, she asked when he'd become a Christian.

"Always have been, just never went to your church." He'd attended Sunday services all across the country, checking out different denominations. "Thing about knowing the Lord is you have friends and family everywhere. You recognize them when you meet them."

She didn't know about church, but she'd found the same rapport in AA meetings. People cared. They didn't use the Christian jargon, but had their own lingo and simple slogans to get through each day. *First things first. Think! Easy does it. Let go and let God.* She'd felt Jesus' presence there. No one looked down at her from the pulpit or told her she wasn't welcome. She could say, "My name is Carolyn and I'm an alcoholic" and hear "Welcome, Carolyn," instead of being shown the door and told not to come back until she had proof of repentance. She would have crashed and burned long ago if she hadn't found a meeting close by.

Mitch ate as though he enjoyed the food. "What was it like in Haight-Ashbury?"

She told him about the pot and alcohol, the constant parties, the confusion and angst. She told him about Woodstock and the long, frightening drive home with Chel still half out of her mind in the backseat. She told him about Ash and his brand of enlightenment, though she left out the drug-induced sexual exploits, the rapes. Some things should be shared only with God and her dead brother.

"Were you in love with him?"

What she'd felt for Ash couldn't be called love. "No. I saw him for who he really was the day Chel died. In a way, her death freed me."

"But you're still not free of all of it, are you?" His eyes filled with compassion. "You're still carrying a truckload of guilt and shame."

She stood and started clearing the table. Mitch helped. He insisted on washing the dishes. She dried and put things away. She thought he would leave then, but he said he'd love a cup of coffee. She apologized for not making a dessert. She'd forgotten. She didn't even have ice cream or store-bought cookies to offer.

He grinned. "We could always go for a ride on my Harley. There's a Baskin-Robbins in Walnut Creek."

She thought of sitting behind him on that powerful bike, her body pressed against his, her arms wrapped around his waist, holding on tight. "I don't think so."

She filled two mugs and carried them back into the living room. She asked him more questions about his travels, about the churches he'd visited, the pastors. He laughed. "Oh, there were a few who took one look at my Harley and black leather jacket and tried to bar the door, but for the most part, I felt welcome." He glanced at the mantel clock. "It's getting late. I'd better go."

She stood, amazed at how quickly five hours had passed. Would he think her too forward if she asked him over again? "When do you head back to Healdsburg?"

"Tomorrow morning."

"Oh." She felt the prick of tears, the sting of loss. "Well, it's been wonderful seeing you, Mitch."

"Thanks for dinner. It's been a great evening." Smiling at her, Mitch shrugged into his black leather jacket. "I'm coming back, Carolyn."

Relieved, she walked him to the door, remembering what he'd

said about never getting over her. Even if that had changed, at least she knew she had a friend.

Mitch put his hand on the doorknob, started to turn it, and then let it go. He turned toward her. He looked uncertain. "Would you mind if I did something I've been dreaming about for years?"

"What?"

"Kiss you."

She caught her breath, but didn't move. He raised his hand tentatively, giving her the opportunity to say no. He cupped her cheek and bent down slowly, still giving her time to decide. She held her breath. When his mouth touched hers, sensation flooded her body. He raised his head and looked into her eyes. "Nice."

He kissed her again. She stepped close, her hands slipping inside his leather jacket. He let out a soft groan, and his arms came around her, fitting her to him. She didn't have to wonder if he was affected. Her body went hot.

She didn't know how long they stood there, bodies straining to get closer, but she didn't want him to stop.

Finally Mitch put a few inches between them. "Better than any fantasy I've ever had." He gave a hoarse laugh and kissed her below the ear. "Nice to know your heart's beating as fast as mine." His breath sent tingles down her spine. When his hands moved over her back, she instinctively arched against him. He set her away from him. "I need to get out of here." He opened the door this time.

"Mitch . . ." She didn't have to say any more.

"If I stay, I won't stop. And then you'll wonder. I don't want you questioning yourself or having any regrets after we're married." He went out.

She stepped out onto the porch. "What did you say?"

"You heard me." He grinned at her as he pulled on his helmet. "I'll call you tomorrow." He swung his leg over and kick-started the motorcycle.

He'd already kick-started her heart; it roared more loudly than his Harley.

21

MITCH CALLED EVERY evening, right after May Flower Dawn had gone to bed. Sometimes they talked until past midnight. He came back every weekend, driving a sedan instead of his Harley so they could include her daughter on Saturday outings. He found activities they all could enjoy: hiking in the hills, a drive into San Francisco to see the Steinhart Aquarium, horseback riding, a base-ball game. Carolyn always offered to fix dinner on Friday night, but Mitch said it'd be safer to go to a restaurant. "I have to keep my hands off you in a public place." He attended church services in Walnut Creek and always invited her. She always refused. She assured him she had her own fellowship to attend. She went to AA meetings every Wednesday night and read the Bible Oma had given her years ago. Sundays were her day of rest, and rest meant staying home and working in the garden while everyone else in her family went to church, including May Flower Dawn.

"Someone really hurt you, didn't they?"

She shrugged. Why tell him the pastor she'd known all her life said she wasn't good enough to enter God's house? Why tell him

Thelma Martin was still a deaconess and Rev. Elias still ruled from the pulpit? What right did she have to judge?

When Mitch invited Carolyn and May Flower Dawn to spend a weekend with him in Alexander Valley, Carolyn agreed. Directions in hand, one small suitcase for herself and another for May Flower Dawn, Carolyn drove up.

She had been prepared for a nice ranch house with a vineyard, but gaped when she turned onto his stone paver driveway and saw the Spanish-style mansion at the end. Mitch came out to welcome them. Opening her door, he helped her out, kissed her, and then frowned. "What's wrong?"

"That." She pointed.

Dawn stood with her mouth gaping. "Do you live here?"

"Yep. Come on. I'll show you around." He took Carolyn's hand.

Her entire house would fit in his family room. The master suite wasn't much smaller. He had a formal parlor living room, four bedrooms with private baths, a kitchen a professional chef would envy, and a solarium with French doors opening to a trellised patio that looked out on terraced gardens, a swimming pool, and a gazebo. She spotted two Hispanic gardeners at work, undoubtedly full-time. She gleaned he had four full-time employees working in the vineyard, more in the winery.

"We can take a look at the operation later, if you'd like."

Carolyn said never mind. She'd already seen enough. He took them back inside the house and asked if Dawn would like to play a video game in the family room. "You have video games!"

Mitch sat with Dawn until she knew how to use the system and play the game, then left her to it. Carolyn stood in the kitchen, taking in the shiny stainless-steel appliances. He touched her arm. "You want a Coke? lemonade?" He gave her a teasing smile. "Well water?"

"Right now, I'd go for an eight-ounce glass of bourbon straight up." She sank onto a suede stool and looked around at the gorgeous granite counters and custom-built cherrywood cabinets, the Mexican tile floor.

"I told you I did well with investments, Carolyn."

"Slight understatement, I'd say. Are you sure you don't have a wife and twelve children hiding somewhere? The place is big enough."

"Only four bedrooms."

Not counting the maid's quarters, complete with kitchen and living room. She didn't know what to say.

He smiled at her as he put a tall glass of iced lemonade in front of her. "I want a family. I tend to plan ahead. I've only ever wanted one wife. You." His eyes warmed. "We're going to make beautiful babies together and have fun doing it."

Fighting down the heat he roused in her so easily, she shook her head. "I don't know, Mitch. I don't have your confidence."

"Yes, you do." He came around the counter, turned her on the stool, and cupped her face. "You knew before I brought you up here." He kissed her firmly. "I'm not letting you chicken out."

❄ ❄ ❄

1978

They'd been talking to one another every night and seeing one another every weekend for six months. Finally, one evening in May, Mitch told Dawn over dinner that he wanted to marry her mother. "How do you feel about that?"

"Does she want to marry you?"

"I think so." He winked at Carolyn. "But I haven't formally asked her yet." He looked back at Dawn. "I wanted your permission first."

"I guess it's okay." Dawn seemed bemused at the idea, and she clearly had no idea how it might change her life. Carolyn wondered if she should explain that it would mean leaving Granny and Papa. It would mean moving away and seeing them only on occasion. Would May Flower Dawn be so indifferent then?

"Maybe we should talk about this later." Carolyn gave Mitch a pleading look. "Alone."

But once alone, talk wasn't uppermost on their minds. "Good thing you brought Dawn with you."

"Our chaperone has been asleep for an hour."

He put his fingers over her mouth. "Don't tempt me. Let's set a date, Carolyn. How much time do you need to put together a church wedding?"

She broke out in a cold sweat. "Why don't we just go to Reno?" A church wedding implied a minister who would be willing to perform the ceremony, a white gown, bridesmaids, flowers, music, a church organ or piano playing, a congregation of witnesses, a reception in the social hall.

"I'm in a hurry, Carolyn, but not that big a hurry. Every woman wants a nice wedding and you're going to have one."

"If that's the condition, the answer is no."

"No? You're in love with me, aren't you?"

"What has love got to do with it? What would I wear, Mitch? Black? Who'd stand up with me? You think my parents would want to foot the bill for my wedding? And who'd want to come?" Fighting tears, she pushed away.

Mitch turned her around, his eyes dark with pain. "I could name a hundred people who'd want to come."

"All *your* friends." No one knew any of hers. AA was an anonymous program. First names only.

"Yours, too. You have more than you realize. I'll bet Candace would jump at the chance to stand up with you. Dawn could be part of the wedding party. I'll pay for it."

"No."

He rubbed her arms. "We'll keep it small—family, friends. Your grandmother, your parents, aunts, uncles, cousins . . . They're going to want to come, Carolyn. You can't cut out the people you love. Only one thing I won't bend on. I want my pastor to perform the ceremony. If you don't want it in a church, okay. We can have it here, in the gazebo. How about August, just before Dawn has to start school?" He held her shoulders. "What do you say?"

When she looked up at him, she knew May was still a month